234 M
41

KISSING CHRISTMAS GOODBYE

ALSO BY M. C. BEATON

Agatha Raisin

Love, Lies and Liquor: An Agatha Raisin Mystery
The Deadly Dance: An Agatha Raisin Mystery
Agatha Raisin and the Haunted House
Agatha Raisin and the Case of the Curious Curate
Agatha Raisin and the Day the Floods Came
Agatha Raisin and the Love from Hell
Agatha Raisin and the Fairies of Fryfam
Agatha Raisin and the Witch of Wyckhadden
Agatha Raisin and the Wizard of Evesham
Agatha Raisin and the Wellspring of Death
Agatha Raisin and the Terrible Tourist
Agatha Raisin and the Murderous Marriage
Agatha Raisin and the Walkers of Dembley
Agatha Raisin and the Potted Gardener
Agatha Raisin and the Vicious Vet
Agatha Raisin and the Quiche of Death ➤

The Skeleton in the Closet

Hamish Macbeth

Death of a Bore
Death of a Poison Pen
Death of a Village
Death of a Celebrity
A Highland Christmas

Writing as Marion Chesney

Our Lady of Pain
Sick of Shadows
Hasty Death
Snobbery with Violence

KISSING CHRISTMAS GOODBYE

An Agatha Raisin Mystery

✝

M. C. BEATON

St. Martin's Minotaur ✖ New York

This is a work of fiction. All of the characters, organizations, and events portrayed in this novel are either products of the author's imagination or are used fictitiously.

ISBN-13: 978-0-312-34911-0
ISBN-10: 0-312-34911-4

KISSING CHRISTMAS GOODBYE

ONE

†

AGATHA RAISIN was bored.

Her detective agency in the English Cotswolds was thriving, but the cases were all small, niggling and unexciting, and yet took a great deal of time to solve. She sometimes felt if she had to deal with another missing cat or dog, she would scream.

Dreams and fantasies, that cushion she usually had against the realities of life, had, to her astonished mind, disappeared entirely. She had dreamed so long about her neighbour and ex-husband, James Lacey, that she would not accept the fact that she did not love him any more. She thought of him angrily as some sort of drug that had ceased to work.

So although it was only early October, she tried to fill her mind with thoughts of Christmas. Unlike quite a number of people, Agatha had not given up on Christmas. To have the perfect Christmas had been a childhood dream whilst surviving a rough upbringing in a Birmingham slum. Holly berries glistened, snow fell gently outside, and inside, all was Dickensian jollity. And in her dreams, James Lacey kissed her under the mistletoe, and, like a middle-aged sleeping beauty, she would awake to passion once more.

Her friend, the vicar's wife, Mrs. Bloxby, had once pointed out that Christmas was to celebrate the birth of Christ, but Agatha's mind shied away from that. To her, Christmas was more Hollywood than church.

Christmas advertisements were already appearing on television, and supermarket aisles were laden with Christmas crackers, mince pies and puddings.

But something happened one crisp morning early in the month to take her mind off Christmas.

She was sitting in her office in Mircester, going through the files with her secretary, Mrs. Freedman, wondering whether to handle another dreary job herself or to turn it over to one of her two detectives, Phil Marshall and Patrick Mulligan. Her erstwhile detective, young Harry Beam, was now studying at Cambridge, and Agatha missed his hard-working energy.

"I nearly forgot," said Mrs. Freedman, "but this letter arrived for you. It's marked 'personal,' so I didn't open it."

Agatha picked it up. The handwriting on the envelope was spidery and there was no return address. She opened it. She read:

Dear Mrs. Raisin,

I have learned of your prowess as a detective through the local newspapers and I wonder if you might find time to call on me. I think a member of my family is trying to kill me. Isn't the weather warm for October?

Yours sincerely,
Phyllis Tamworthy

The paper was expensive. The address in raised italic script at the top gave the address of the Manor House, Lower Tapor, Gloucestershire.

"Nuts," said Agatha. "Barking mad. How are our profits?"

"Good," said Mrs. Freedman. "It is amazing how grateful people are to get one of their pets back."

"I miss Harry," sighed Agatha. "Phil and Patrick don't mind the divorces, but they do hate searching for animals. They think it's all beneath them, and I think it's beneath me."

"Why don't you employ a young person to cope with the missing animals? A girl, perhaps. Girls are very keen on animals."

"That's a very good idea. Put an ad in the local paper and we'll see if we can get anyone. Say we want a trainee."

A week later, Agatha, after a long day of interviews, felt she would never, ever find someone suitable. It seemed as if all the dimmest girls in Mircester fancied themselves as detectives. Some had come dressed in black leather and stiletto-heeled boots, thinking that a Charlie's Angels image would be appropriate. Unfortunately, with the exception of one anorexic, the rest were overweight with great bosoms and buttocks. Weight would not have mattered, however, if any of them had shown the least spark of intelligence.

Agatha was about to pack up for the day when the door to her office opened and a young girl entered. She had blonde hair that looked natural and pale-blue eyes fringed with thick fair lashes in a neat-featured face. She was conservatively dressed in a tailored suit, white blouse and low-heeled shoes.

"Yes?" asked Agatha.

"My name is Toni Gilmour. I believe you are looking for a trainee detective."

"Applicants are supposed to apply in writing."

"I know. But you see, I've just made up my mind to try for the job."

Actually, Toni had been lurking in the street outside for a good part of the day, studying the girls who came out after their interviews, examining their faces and listening to what they said. She gathered that no one had got the job. She deliberately calculated that if she turned up last, then a desperate Mrs. Raisin might take her on.

But Agatha was anxious to get home to her cats and relax for the weekend.

"Go away and write your application," she said. "Send in copies of your school certificates plus a short description of why you think you might be suited for the job."

Agatha half-rose from her seat behind her desk but sat down again as Toni said, "I have brought my school certificates with me. I am well educated. I work hard. People like me. I feel that is important in getting facts."

Agatha scowled at her. Agatha's way of getting facts was usually either by lying or emotional blackmail or outright bullying.

"It's not glamorous," said Agatha. "Your job will be to try

to find missing dogs and cats. It's tedious work and you will often find that the animal has been killed on the road or has probably been stolen. When did you leave school?"

"Last June. I'm seventeen."

"Are you employed at the moment?"

"Yes, I work at the pharmacy counter at Shalbeys." Shalbeys was one of the local supermarkets. "I work the late shift."

"The difficulty is that I need someone to start right away."

"That's all right," said Toni. "I can get the sack."

"Don't you want to go to university?"

"I can't bear the idea of having a bank loan for my studies around my neck for years. Mrs. Raisin, it would do no harm to give me a trial."

"I don't like the idea of you trying to get the sack. You'll be letting your employers down."

"There are plenty of girls to take my place. I think I am showing initiative. You cannot want a detective who plays by the rules the whole time."

Agatha realized how tired she was. Toni had a clear, precise manner of speaking, hardly ever heard in the local youth these days, where the glottal stop was considered de rigueur.

"All right. Report here on Monday morning at nine o'clock. You'd better wear flat shoes and clothes you don't mind getting messed up."

"How much will I be paid?" asked Toni.

"Six pounds an hour and no overtime while you are a trainee. But do well and I'll give you a bonus. You may claim reasonable expenses."

Toni thanked her and left.

"Odd girl," commented Agatha.

"I thought she was nice," said Mrs. Freedman. "Quite old-fashioned."

Toni cycled to her home in one of Mircester's worst housing estates. She pushed her bike up the weedy garden path and propped it against the wall of the house. Then she took a deep breath and let herself in. Her brother, Terry, was sitting slumped in front of the television with a bottle of beer in one hand and a fish supper in the other. "Where's Mum?" asked Toni.

"Passed out," said Terry. Unlike his slim sister, Terry was a mass of bulging muscles. A scar from a knife fight in a pub marred his right cheek.

Toni went upstairs and looked in her mother's bedroom. Mrs. Gilmour was lying fully clothed on top of the bed. An empty vodka bottle lay on the bed beside her. The air stank of sweat and booze.

Toni went to her own room and took off the suit she had borrowed from a friend. She hung the suit away carefully and then put on jeans and a clean T-shirt.

Downstairs, she took down a denim jacket from a peg on the wall and put it on. She opened the door and began to wheel her bike back down the garden.

Her brother appeared in the doorway behind her. "Where you goin'?" he shouted.

"Work. Late shift," yelled Toni. "Remember that stuff called work? Why don't you get yourself a job, you wanker?"

Agatha was about to put a packaged curry into the microwave for her dinner when the doorbell rang. When she opened her front door she saw her friend Mrs. Bloxby carrying a box of books.

"These books were left after the sale at the church," said Mrs. Bloxby. "They're the old green-and-white Penguin detective stories. I thought you might like to have them."

"Suits me fine. Come in and put them on the kitchen table. I plan a lazy weekend and you've saved me a trip to the bookshop."

Mrs. Bloxby sat down at the kitchen table. Agatha looked at her friend with sudden concern. The vicar's wife looked tired. The lines under her gentle eyes were more pronounced, and strands of wispy grey hair were escaping from the bun at the base of her neck.

"Let me get you a sherry," said Agatha. "You look worn-out."

"Alf has a cold," said Mrs. Bloxby. Alf was the vicar. Agatha always thought Alf was a stupid name for a vicar. He ought to have been called Peregrine or Clarence or Digby or something like that. "I've been doing the parish visits for him. Honestly, half of them don't even bother coming to church."

Agatha placed a glass of sherry in front of her.

"I don't suppose anyone's frightened of God any more," commented Agatha. "People like a good fright."

"Cynical, but true," said Mrs. Bloxby. "Ecology is the new religion. The planet is dying, the poles are melting, and it's all your fault, you sinners. Did you get a girl for your dogs and cats?"

"I'm trying someone out. She's neat and clean and somewhat old-fashioned in her speech and manner. Odd, these days."

*   *   *

7

"You're always trying to brush against my boobs, you old perv," Toni was saying to the pharmacist, Basil Jones.

"There's not much space here," said Basil, outraged. "I was merely trying to get past you." Basil's anger was fuelled by the fact that he *had* deliberately brushed against her.

"You're nothin' but a sad old sack," said Toni.

Basil's face was now mottled with anger. "You're fired!"

"Okey-dokey," said Toni cheerfully.

"Have you heard from Mr. Lacey?" Mrs. Bloxby asked.

"No, he's gone off somewhere. Don't care. Though if he comes back in time, I might invite him to my Christmas dinner."

"Oh, no, Mrs. Raisin! Not again!"

Agatha had previously had a disaster of a Christmas dinner when she had used the oven in the church hall to cook an enormous turkey, turned the gas up too high and filled the hall with acrid black smoke.

"It'll be perfect this time!" Both Agatha and Mrs. Bloxby called each other by their second names, an old-fashioned custom in the Carsely Ladies' Society, to which they both belonged.

"It's only October," said the vicar's wife plaintively. "No one should be allowed to mention Christmas before the first of December."

Agatha grinned. "You'll see. I'll have it one week before, so it won't interfere with anyone's family arrangements."

Mrs. Bloxby finished her sherry and rose wearily to her feet. "I'll drive you to the vicarage," said Agatha.

"Nonsense. I can walk."

"I insist," said Agatha.

The vicar was sitting reading a book with a box of tissues on a table beside him. "Hullo, dear," he said faintly.

"How are you?" asked Agatha briskly.

"Still very weak."

"Your wife is exhausted," said Agatha, "so I'm going to look after you and give her a break."

He looked at Agatha in horror. "There's no need. In fact, I'm feeling better by the minute."

"We can't have your wife falling ill with overwork, now can we?" Agatha gave him a wide smile, but her small bearlike eyes were threatening. The vicar turned to his wife. "Please go and lie down, dearest. I assure you I am now well enough to fix us a light supper. *Mrs. Raisin, your services will not be needed!*"

"Alf, you're shouting," protested Mrs. Bloxby. "Mrs. Raisin was only just trying to help."

Agatha drove back to her cottage with a grin on her face. Men, she thought. Typical. Women get colds and men get flu.

After dinner, she took the box of books through to her sitting room. She selected a detective story by Marjorie Allingham and began to read. The next day, she chose one by Edmund Crispin and followed that up with one by Freeman Willis Croft. She was fishing in her handbag for her cigarettes when her fingers touched an envelope. She drew it out. It was that odd letter from Mrs. Tamworthy. Agatha, her mind full of detective stories, reread the letter with new eyes.

What if the threat to this woman was real? Perhaps she would be invited to stay. Mrs. Tamworthy would be an elegant silver-haired aristocratic lady. She would have a plump, pompous son with a bitchy wife. Her daughter would be the gruff, hunting sort who had never married. She would have one fey granddaughter, very beautiful, engaged to an actor; and another granddaughter, a straightforward no-nonsense girl who was secretly in love with the actor and . . .

The telephone rang shrilly, interrupting her fantasy.

The call was from Roy Silver, a young man who had once worked for Agatha when she had owned a public relations firm.

"How's things?" asked Roy.

"Cruising along. What about you?" Roy now worked for the public relations firm that had bought Agatha's business.

"I'm pushing a new perfume. It's called Green Desire. It's made by an Irish company."

"Any good?"

"I'll bring you a bottle." There was a pause. "As a matter of fact, I took the liberty of driving down."

"Where are you?"

"Round the corner."

"Come along, then."

Agatha went to her front door, opened it and waited for Roy. It was unlike him to arrive unexpectedly. He always wanted something. He was probably having trouble with the Green Desire account.

Roy drove up, got out, opened the boot and dragged out a large suitcase.

"Going somewhere on holiday?" asked Agatha.

"Here, if you'll have me, sweetie."

"Roy, wait a minute. This is a bit of an imposition."

To her horror, Roy burst into tears. His thin body in his Armani suit shook with sobs, and tears trickled down through his designer stubble.

"Bring that case in," ordered Agatha, "and I'll fix you a stiff drink."

She told him to leave his case in the hall, led the way into the sitting room and poured him a strong measure of brandy from the drinks trolley. "Here, get that down you," she ordered. "Don't wipe your nose on your sleeve. There's a box of tissues on the table."

Roy sank down onto the sofa. He blew his nose vigorously, took a swig of brandy, and then stared miserably into space.

Agatha joined him on the sofa. "Now, then, out with it."

"It's been an Irish nightmare," said Roy. "I'm all broken up. I've handled nasty drug-ridden pop groups and prima-donna models, but never anything like this."

"Who's producing the stuff? The IRA?"

"No, it's a Dublin fashion house called Colleen Donnelly. They decided to launch into the perfume market. They wanted it pushed as a 'family' perfume, the sort of thing you could give to your old granny. So the publicity shots were taken in various front parlours out in the bogs with gran, mam, dad, and the kids. It's been going on for months. I am awash with tea and boredom. I thought if I had to listen to someone's uncle stand in front of the fire and sing 'Danny Boy' just one more time, I would scream."

"Should have been a joy to promote," said Agatha.

"Sounds as if it would lend itself to some good photos for the glossies."

"Oh, I got them a good show. It's not that. It's Colleen Donnelly herself. She isn't Irish. She's from Manchester. Real name, Betty Clap."

"You can see why she'd want to change her name."

"She's a bitch. She's the worst bitch I've ever worked for and that includes you, Aggie."

"Here, wait just one minute—"

"Sorry. She turned up the whole time, jeering at me in front of the camera crew and everyone, calling me a wimp and a half-man. I told the boss, Mr. Pedman, but he said it was a big launch and to stick with it. Then, just before the final big launch party, she phoned the agency and asked for another public relations officer. She said . . . she said, she was sick of dealing with a twittering idiot. He sent Mary Hartley."

"Who's she?"

"Some cow who's jealous of me and has always been trying to steal my accounts. I'm a failure. I can't bear it. I had holiday owing, so I just took off in the car and I found myself driving towards you."

"Have you got a bottle of the stuff with you?"

Roy fished in his pocket and pulled out a green glass bottle with a gold stopper. Agatha took off the top and dabbed a little on her wrist.

"It's lousy, Roy."

"But it'll get good publicity and all because of me, and Mary will take the credit."

Agatha handed him the television remote control. "You sit there and finish your drink and watch something silly. I'll see what I can do."

Agatha went into her study and logged on to her computer. She opened the file which held all her old journalist contacts. Then she switched off and picked up the phone and called Deirdre Dunn, top woman's editor on *The Bugle.* To her relief, Deirdre was working late.

"What is it, Agatha?" asked Deirdre. "I thought you were into the detective business."

"I am. But I want you to do me a favour and knock a perfume called Green Desire."

"Why should I?"

"Remember I accidentally found out you were having an affair with the foreign secretary, Peter Branson?"

"Do you have to rake that up?"

"Only if necessary."

"All right, you old whore. What am I supposed to do?"

"Take this down."

Twenty minutes later, Agatha returned to the sitting room. "All fixed," she said cheerfully.

"What is?" demanded Roy.

"Deirdre Dunn is putting a piece in the Sunday edition of *The Bugle,* saying that Green Desire is one crap perfume, despite the brilliant public relations work of one Roy Silver, whom the thankless Betty Clap betrayed with her lack of business acumen by firing him at the last minute and exchanging him for someone with considerably less experience. She's also sending her assistant out into the streets to do a vox pop, spraying people with the stuff and asking them what they think of it. She'll only print the bad comments. Deirdre has great power. The stuff's doomed. Revenge is thine."

"I don't know how to thank you, Agatha. How did you persuade Deirdre?"

"Oh, we go back a long way. We're great friends."

Roy looked at Agatha uneasily. Deirdre, all skeletal elegance and cut-glass voice, had once said to him that if Agatha ever died, she would cheerfully piss on her grave.

"Will it work?" he asked.

"Trust me."

"Well, thanks, Aggie. How can I repay you?"

"Just don't stay too long."

Agatha came down to the kitchen the next morning to find a plate of fresh croissants on the table, and Roy sitting reading the newspapers.

"Where did you get the croissants?" she asked.

"The village shop. Some woman in the village has started making them. I've made coffee."

Agatha opened the back door and let her cats out to play. She poured herself a cup of coffee, sat down at the table and lit a cigarette.

"Must you?" asked Roy, flapping his hands.

"Yes, so shut up." Agatha saw she had left Mrs. Tamworthy's letter lying on the table. She handed it to Roy. "Read that and tell me what you think about it."

Roy read it carefully. "She sounds mad."

"She might not be. I might read about her death in the newspapers and feel guilty."

"It's a nice day," said Roy. The morning mist was lifting.

Agatha's cats, Hodge and Boswell, were chasing each other over the lawn. "We could both go over and talk to her."

"Wouldn't do any harm," said Agatha. "That way we'll find out whether she's bonkers or not."

TWO

†

THEY EVENTUALLY found Lower Tapor after having become lost several times. Signposts seemed to ignore the very existence of the place. Neither Roy nor Agatha were much good at reading maps, and so it was by accident that they at last found themselves confronted by a sign announcing Lower Tapor.

They drove slowly between two rows of small red brick cottages and then found themselves out of the village at the other end.

"Snakes and bastards!" muttered Agatha, executing a clumsy eight-point turn. Back again. "Look for someone," hissed Agatha.

But the street appeared deserted. "Look!" said Roy. "There's that little road on the left. It must lead somewhere."

Agatha whipped the wheel round and plunged down the side road. They came to a triangle of village green with houses set around it and one pub called The Crazy Fox.

Agatha stopped the car outside the pub. They both got out and stood for a moment looking up at the inn sign, which displayed a painting of a fox dressed as a huntsman, gun in hand, standing upright with one rear paw resting on the dead body of a man.

The pub itself was a low building built of mellow Cotswold stone. The village was very quiet. The day was perfect and the sun warm.

Agatha pushed open the door and, followed by Roy, went inside. She stood and blinked in surprise. The pub was full of people. A man with a clipboard stood in front of the bar. He had been addressing the crowd but fell silent and stared at Agatha.

"What do you want?" he asked.

"I want directions to the Manor House," retorted Agatha.

There was a sudden uneasy rustling of papers and whispering voices.

"Why?" demanded the man with the clipboard. He was a big, burly farming type and his small eyes were suddenly full of menace.

"Because that's where I'm trying to get to," howled Agatha.

"Go out. Turn right, and down Badger Lane. Takes you there."

"Any chance of a drink?" asked Roy.

"No," said the man. "This is a private meeting. Get out."

"Well I never!" said Roy, outside.

"Oh, forget about the local yokels," said Agatha. "Let's find this house."

They got back into the car and found Badger Lane leading off from a corner of the green. Agatha drove slowly. The lane ran between high stone walls and was so narrow she was afraid of scraping her car.

"There it is," she said, spotting a double gate on which hung a small sign, MANOR HOUSE.

"You'd better get out and open the gates," said Agatha.

"Why me?" complained Roy.

"Because I'm driving."

Grumbling, Roy got out. He was soon back. "The gates are padlocked. We should have phoned first. Phone now."

"No, I want to surprise her," said Agatha. "I want to find out if she's really bonkers. We'll leave the car here and climb over the gate."

"It might be a farm," said Roy uneasily, looking at the fields of wheat that stretched out on either side of a road on the other side of the gate. "We could walk miles."

"Don't be such a wimp. Come on."

As Agatha climbed over the gate, her hip gave a nasty twinge. She had been told she had arthritis in her right hip and would need a hip replacement. She had gone back to her Pilates classes earlier in the year but had recently stopped going.

Thankful that she had put on a trouser suit and flat shoes, Agatha began to trudge along the road.

After two miles of walking, her feet were aching and her bad hip was throbbing.

"It must be here somewhere," she said, exasperated. "There are some trees up ahead. Might be there."

But when they reached the trees it was to find another sign, on a post this time, with the legend MANOR HOUSE picked out in gold paint. Ahead of them lay a metalled driveway.

Glad to be under the shade of the trees, they walked on. The road twisted and turned, thickly wooded on either side.

"We've been walking for hours," groaned Roy.

After what seemed an age, they arrived at a lodge house and could see the road stretching on between two fields, where sheep cropped the grass, to buildings at the top of a rise.

"Nearly there," said Agatha. Now she was beginning to wish she had phoned instead. Her linen trouser suit was beginning to stick to her back and she knew her face was shiny.

Roy was consoled by the thought of all the weight he must be losing. Although skinny, he believed one could never be thin enough.

They passed some well-ordered stables, turned a corner and found the house at last. It was a square Georgian house with a porticoed entrance and one long Victorian wing to one side.

"It's very quiet," said Roy. "What if she was down at that meeting in the pub?"

"We're here anyway. May as well ring the bell."

They rang the bell and waited. At last the door was opened by a small, stout, motherly-looking woman wearing an old-fashioned flowery pinafore over a black dress.

"We have come to see your mistress," said Agatha grandly.

"That being?"

"Mrs. Tamworthy, of course."

"You've found her. I'm Mrs. Tamworthy."

Agatha flushed with embarrassment. A drop of sweat ran down her cheek. "I am so sorry. I am Agatha Raisin. You wrote to me."

"So I did. Come in."

They followed her across a hall and into a large airy sitting room overlooking a vista of lawns and an ornamental lake.

"Sit down," ordered Mrs. Tamworthy. "Drink?"

"Please," said Agatha. "Gin and tonic, if you have it."

"Beer for me," said Roy, and Agatha looked at him in surprise. She had never known Roy to drink beer.

Mrs. Tamworthy went to a drinks cupboard in the corner. "You live a long way from the village," said Agatha. "We had quite a walk. The gates are padlocked."

"You never come that long way! You should have come through Upper Tapor. The gates on that side are always open and only a few yards off the road."

There was a little refrigerator under the drinks cupboard. Agatha soon heard the welcome tinkle of ice being dropped in a glass.

"Drinks are ready," called Mrs. Tamworthy. They both rose to their feet, Agatha wincing as she did so.

When they were all seated again, Agatha asked, "Who is trying to kill you?"

"One of the family will try, I think. They are all coming here next Saturday for my eightieth birthday."

"Eighty! You don't look it."

"It's one of the benefits of being fat, my dear. It stretches the wrinkles."

Agatha noticed for the first time that Mrs. Tamworthy's hair, worn in a French pleat, was dyed brown. There were deep wrinkles around her eyes but her cheeks were smooth. Her eyes were small and black, the kind of eyes which are good at concealing the owner's feelings. She was very small, very round, with only the vestige of a waist. Her feet, encased in flat slippers, did not meet the floor.

Agatha took a strong swallow of gin and tonic, opened her handbag and took out a pen and notebook.

"Why should one of your family want to kill you?"

"Because I'm selling this place, lock, stock and barrel, and that includes the village."

"Why should they object?"

"Because they all want to go on like lords of the manor. You see the portraits of my ancestors on the wall?"

Agatha looked round. "Yes."

"All fake. That was my daughter Sadie's idea. Ashamed of the family background because she's married to that stuffed shirt Sir Henry Field. Now, my late husband, he made his money in building bricks. He started work as a brickie, but he won the football pools, and the brickyard was going bust so he bought it. Then the housing boom came along and he made a fortune. Our children, there are four of them—two sons, Bert and Jimmy, and two girls, Sadie and Fran. They all got good educations. Sadie and Fran were sent to a finishing school in Switzerland and that's where they got their grand ideas. My husband, Hugh, would have done anything for them, and just after they had nagged him into buying this estate, he died of cancer. I took over the business and doubled his fortune, got a good manager for this estate who actually ran the farms at a profit.

"They even made me take elocution lessons. But I want my own life now. I never liked it here. I want a small flat of my own."

"Why not just leave the estate to your children?"

"They'd run it into the ground. My Hugh didn't work hard just for me to see it all frittered away."

"But one of them wanting to kill you!" exclaimed Agatha. "Are you sure?"

"You'd better come along to my birthday party and see them for yourself."

"I don't come as a detective, do I?"

"No, you say you're a friend of mine. You can bring your son as well."

"He is not my son," said Agatha angrily. "He used to work for me."

"Bring a bag. You'd better stay the weekend."

"I'll get my secretary to send you a contract outlining fees and expenses," said Agatha. "Now, is your other daughter, Fran, married?"

"Was. Didn't work out. Divorced."

"Why didn't it work out?"

"Husband, Larry, was a stockbroker. Pompous prat. Fran says he thought she was common and it was all my fault. She blames me for the divorce."

"And your sons?"

"Bert is a darling but weak. He manages the brickworks. He married a farmer's daughter, or rather she married him."

"Name?"

"Alison."

"What's she like?"

"All four-wheel drives, tweeds, sounds like the queen. A bully."

"And Jimmy?"

Phyllis Tamworthy's face softened. "Ah, my Jimmy. He's a dear. Quiet and decent."

"What are the ages of your children?"

"Sadie is fifty-eight, Fran, fifty-six, Bert, fifty-two and my Jimmy is forty. I thought I was past it when he came along."

"And grandchildren?"

"Only two. There's Fran's daughter, Annabelle. She's thirty-seven, and Sadie's daughter, Lucy, is thirty-two."

"And do they have children?"

"Just Lucy. Her child, Jennifer, is eight."

Agatha scribbled busily in her notebook.

Roy piped up. "Which one of them do you think is going to kill you?"

"I don't know. It's just a feeling I have."

Agatha raised her eyes from her notebook. "You're not telling us everything. You've a pretty good idea of who it might be. You seem a sensible woman. You don't just have feelings about things."

"You're the detective. I'm hiring you to find out."

Roy, again. "We went into the village pub to ask for directions and there seemed to be some sort of meeting going on there."

"Oh, they're always complaining about something. I own the village as well. There was a Sir Mark Riptor owned this place before my husband bought it. When I took over, they asked me to donate thirty thousand pounds to the upkeep of the cricket club because Sir Mark had always looked after them. I refused. Then they wanted the village fête here. Sir Mark always had it. I refused. They said there had always been a fête at the manor since time immemorial. I said, 'Tough.' So they have meetings and grumble. 'Come into the twenty-first century,' I told them. 'I don't expect you to pull your forelocks and act like peasants, so don't expect me to act like the lady of the manor. Shove off.'"

Agatha stared at her. "Don't you think one of them might have it in for you?"

She laughed. "No. They like grumbling."

"How long do you want me to work on this case?"

"The weekend should be enough. I said I was putting the place up for sale right after my eightieth birthday."

"But apart from wanting to keep it as a family home," said Agatha, "won't they inherit a great deal of money from you? I mean, this estate must be worth a mint."

"They won't inherit much. I had to stand on my own two feet and run the business. They should learn to do the same. I'm going to have a technical college built and dedicate it to the memory of my Hugh."

"And do they know this?"

"Yes, I told them a few months ago."

"Did you ever make a will leaving them anything?"

"Yes, I left everything to be divided equally amongst the four of them."

"And have you changed that will?"

"I'm going to change it next week to make sure that college is built. As soon as this place is sold, I shall start the building of the technical college. I am in good health and want to see the work completed before I die. If there's anything left over, they can have it."

"But they can inherit the technical college!"

"No, I'm leaving that to the state."

Agatha took a deep breath. "Are you tired of living?"

"Not a bit."

"Look, under these circumstances, if you were my mother, I might be tempted to kill you myself. Do your children love you?"

"I suppose. Jimmy does."

"What does Jimmy do?"

"He owns a newsagent's and general store in Upper Tapor. I bought it for him so he'll be all right."

"Did he want a shop?"

"The poor lamb is very shy. He didn't know what he wanted to do. I said a shop was the idea. Meet the public. Get out of himself. I hope I've given you enough information because I'm tired and would like to lie down."

"Have you got anyone who could run us back to our car?"

"You'll find Jill, the groom, in the stables. Ask her. Now if you don't mind . . ."

Jill was a cheerful young woman. She said, sure, she'd run them back, and soon they were jolting down the drive in an old Land Rover. "Does Mrs. Tamworthy keep many horses?" shouted Agatha over the roar of the engine.

"No, not her. She rents the stables out to people in the local hunt. Makes a lot."

Agatha fell silent. She kept wondering why Mrs. Tamworthy had put herself in so much danger.

When she was driving Roy back to Carsely, she asked, "What are you going to do with yourself next week while I'm at work?"

"Lead a healthy lifestyle. Go for walks."

"You'll get bored."

"I doubt it. I'll be so busy wondering about this birthday party. It's all very weird. Like an old-fashioned detective story."

"Don't worry," said Agatha. "Nothing will happen. I've come to the conclusion that she really is a bit unbalanced."

Sunday was a wearisome day for Agatha and several times

she considered going into the office just to get away from an ecstatic Roy, who had bought ten copies of *The Bugle* and who kept reading out bits of the damning story on Green Desire.

Toni turned up promptly for work on Monday morning. She was looking forward to her new job. She had no illusions about the detective work she would be doing, but she could make her own hours and be her own boss, and that appealed to her.

"Now," said Agatha, "we've got an odd case here." She told them about Mrs. Tamworthy. Then she said, "Patrick, I'd like you to go to that pub in Lower Tapor and find out just how angry the locals are and who the ringleader is. Phil, I'd like you to go to a newsagent's in Upper Tapor and get me an idea of what Jimmy Tamworthy is like. Running a shop was his mother's idea. If my mother was rich and possessed a large estate, I might think running a village shop was beneath me. See if you can get some idea. After that, I'd like you to check out applications for planning permission. I can't see the villagers getting so hot under the collar if she was just going to sell the village. They might hope for a more generous benefactor. But Mrs. Tamworthy likes making money. What if she hoped to get planning permission for more houses? Or planning permission for something the villagers would hate?

"Also, Patrick, while you're in the pub, get an idea of what the locals really think about Mrs. Tamworthy. Any scandal. Do they think she's mad? That sort of thing."

"There's that divorce case," said Patrick. "We really should wrap it up. Mrs. Horrington is paying a lot. Then there's the one Phil is on. Mr. Constable."

26

"I'll take Horrington. I can't be seen near that village before next weekend. I'm going as a friend of the family." Agatha turned round and looked at Toni, who was sitting quietly on the visitor's sofa. She was wearing clean jeans, a white T-shirt and sandals.

"Toni, I'm going to throw you in at the deep end. Can you take photographs?"

"Yes, I was in my camera club at school."

"Phil will give you the Constable file and a camera. Have you a car?"

"I'm too young for a driving licence. I've got a bike."

"That'll do. No one will suspect a teenager on a bike of spying on them."

Phil handed Toni a file. Goodness, he was old, thought Toni. Must be in his seventies, though he seemed fit enough. "It's the usual thing," said Phil, sitting down on the sofa beside her. "The husband, Mr. Constable, thinks his wife, Hetty, is having an affair. I'd only just started following her at the end of last week. There's the address. It's out in the northern end of Mircester, where all the big villas are. But just at the end of the street is a supermarket with a big car park. If you go to the end of the car park, you can get a good view of the house because it's the one nearest the supermarket.

"She drives a BMW, so I hope you can chase her on a pushbike."

"The traffic's so bad in Mircester, I should be able to keep her in view," said Toni.

"Right. I'll give you a camera and a telescopic lens and a camera bag. The equipment is expensive, so take care of it. I'll also give you a small powerful tape recorder in case you get close enough to her to record anything."

Toni's heart began to thump against her ribs. Mrs. Freedman, who felt sympathetic in a motherly way to the young girl, had told her that morning just before Agatha arrived, that her predecessor, Harry, had found a lot of cats and dogs at the animal shelter and had never told Agatha the reason for his successes. So Toni had been looking forward to an easy first day.

As Toni peddled in the direction of the supermarket, she wondered nervously how she was supposed to remain unnoticed standing at the edge of a car park with a telescopic lens fitted to a camera.

She had an idea. When she got to the supermarket, she went in and bought a packet of chocolate chip cookies and a packet of sandwich bags. Outside, she tipped the cookies into a sandwich bag and sealed it. Then she got straight back on her bike and peddled up to Mrs. Constable's house.

She rang the bell. She would say she was selling cookies for the Girl Guides. That way she would find out what her quarry looked like.

When the door opened, Toni stared at the woman looking at her. "Mrs. Mackenzie! What are you doing here?" Mrs. Mackenzie was her next-door neighbour.

"I'm cleaning, that's what."

"Is Mrs. Constable in?"

"No, she's out."

Toni took a deep breath. "Can I talk to you?"

"I was just about to take a break. Come in. We'll have a cuppa."

Toni followed her through to the kitchen. "I've never seen

a kitchen like this outside of advertisements," she marvelled. "It's huge."

"Fortunately for me, madam doesn't do any cooking, or hardly ever. She eats carrot sticks at home or dines out. So what is it, Toni, love? How do you know her?"

"I don't," said Toni, and then plunged in, telling Mrs Mackenzie all about the detective job and how she had to find proof that Mrs. Constable was having an affair.

"Oh, she's having an affair all right, and with a right bit of rough."

"How do you know?"

"I've got the keys, see. I'd left some shopping by mistake one day and came back. I opened the door quiet-like, and went to the kitchen. They were hard at it on the kitchen floor."

"Do you know the chap's name?"

"No—I didn't see his face, neither, only his great hairy bum."

"It would mean a lot if I could get a photograph," said Toni.

"I don't like her and that's a fact," said Mrs. Mackenzie. "Get her out of the way and I'd get peace and quiet just cleaning for Mr. Constable. He's ever so nice."

"Maybe I could hide in the back garden and hope she and her pal choose the kitchen again," said Toni.

"Here, have your tea and get out of here in case she comes back sudden-like. I don't want to know any more about what you're going to do and you never heard a word from me, mind."

"Sure."

Toni drank her tea rapidly, thanked Mrs. Mackenzie and left. But she wheeled her bike round to the back garden and hid it in some bushes. Then she crouched down below the kitchen window and waited.

Fortunately, the garden was surrounded by a high fence and bordering trees and could not be overlooked from any of the neighbouring houses.

Toni waited. And waited. The garden grew hot. After an hour she heard the front door slam. She hoped it was Mrs. Constable returning home, but then she realized it was probably only Mrs. Mackenzie leaving. She opened the sandwich bag and took out a cookie. The chocolate had melted and stuck to her fingers. How odd that chocolate chip biscuits were the only ones in England called "cookies."

Then, at two in the afternoon, when she was feeling so cramped and thirsty she was about to give up, she heard voices coming from the kitchen. The kitchen window was thrust open. "Christ, it's hot in here" came a female voice.

A deep man's voice said, "Then take 'em off, darlin'."

Toni extracted the camera and slowly rose until she could peer in the window. A burly man was unbuttoning a tall blonde woman's blouse while she fumbled at the belt of his jeans. "Come on. Hurry up," he said. They fell to the floor.

He began soon to emit loud grunts, covering the noise of the busy click of the camera shutter. Toni took out the recorder and recorded every obscenity that was pouring out of their mouths.

Feeling slightly sick, Toni quietly lifted her bike from the bushes and made her way silently round the side of the house.

Her friends at school had watched pornography on their computers and she had seen some of it herself. But, she reflected, it was pretty disgusting being a witness to the real thing.

She peddled away as fast as she could, stopping at last at a café where she ordered a sustaining meal of egg and chips and two Cokes.

Then she went back to the office.

Agatha was reading some correspondence. She looked up when Toni came in. "Too hot?" she asked. "I gave up myself."

"No, I've got the photographs."

"Good heavens! Print them off and let's have a look. There's a machine over there. I don't know how to work it. Do you?"

"Yes." Toni printed off the photographs and handed them to Agatha. "I have a tape recording as well." She switched it on. Mrs. Freedman put her hands over her ears.

"That's enough," said Agatha sharply. "Well done. But I didn't expect a young girl like you to be exposed to such filth. I'm sorry. How did you manage to get these?"

Toni told her.

When she had finished, Agatha said, "I can't in all honesty pay you trainee wages for work like this. We'll negotiate a contract for you tomorrow. You may take the rest of the day off. Mrs. Freedman, call Mr. Constable."

"What about Phil's camera?"

"Take it home and bring it back tomorrow."

THREE

✝

AGATHA RETURNED home slightly jealous of young Toni's early success. The girl had luck on her side and Agatha knew that a lucky detective was often a lot more valuable than an experienced one.

Her cats came running to meet her. The house felt silent. "Roy!" she called. She went into the kitchen. There was a note on the kitchen table propped up against a dirty coffee cup.

"Dear Aggie," she read. "Thanks to that brilliant article, I got the Meery baby products account, which is BIG BIG BIG! Sorry I had to dash off. Lots of love, Roy."

Roy must have phoned his boss, thought Agatha, to crow over the article. She had a feeling that he would not be back for the weekend and she would be left on her own to cope with the case.

She fed her cats and let them out into the garden. Although

the day had been unseasonably warm, there was now a slight chill in the air.

She fixed herself a gin and tonic and sat down at the kitchen table feeling lonely.

Her mobile phone rang. At first she couldn't make out who it was because of the gulps and sobs coming down the line. "Take a deep breath, whoever you are," snapped Agatha.

"It's T-Toni," stammered the voice. "He's pinched the camera."

"Who has?"

"M-my b-brother, Terry. He says he's going to sell it in the morning. He's drunk."

"Where are you?"

"I'm locked in my room. He beat me."

"What's your address? I've left it at the office."

Toni gave it to her, along with directions.

"Stay in your room," ordered Agatha. "I'm coming."

"He'll kill you!" wailed Toni. "He's drunk."

"Just wait."

Agatha got into her car and drove to the pub. She said to the barman, John Fletcher, "I need some muscle. Someone's beat up one of my assistants. Anyone want to make some money?"

"I'll see." John lifted the flap of the bar and went over to where two men were eating lasagne and chips and bent over them. Then he came back to Agatha. "How much?"

"A hundred pounds each," said Agatha.

He went back and returned with the men. He introduced them as Dale and Sean. They were agricultural labourers.

As she drove them towards Mircester, Agatha outlined the

problem. "I don't want any broken bones," she warned them. "Just overpower him while I get that camera and get Toni out of there."

"You didn't want to call the police?" asked Sean.

Agatha realized that she could easily have called the police, but perhaps this Terry would lie and say he had only taken the camera as a joke. Toni would be asked if she wanted to press charges and probably wouldn't want to land her brother in prison.

"No, it's better this way," she said.

A faded, drunken woman answered the door to them. "Mrs. Gilmour?" asked Agatha.

"Yesh, what is it?"

"We would like to speak to your son."

"I dunno . . ."

"Let us past," ordered Agatha.

She stood aside, hanging on to the edge of the door for support. Agatha heard the sounds of the television. "In here," she ordered.

Terry was slumped on the sofa with a can of beer.

"I want that camera and lens," said Agatha.

"Dunno what yer talkin' about."

Agatha nodded to Sean and Dale. The two powerful labourers jerked Terry to his feet and slammed him up against the wall.

Mrs. Gilmour staggered into the room. "Leave my baby alone!" she screamed. "I'll call the perleece."

"Do that," said Agatha coldly, "and I'll have your son charged with theft and actual bodily harm."

Sean twisted Terry's arm up his back. "It's in the bag on the floor," he howled. "You're hurting me."

Agatha recognized the camera bag Phil had given Toni. She opened it up and saw the camera and lens were inside.

"Keep him there," she ordered. Mrs. Gilmour had collapsed, weeping, onto the sofa.

Agatha ran up the stairs, shouting, "Toni!" Toni unlocked her bedroom door. She had a cut lip and what looked like the beginnings of a black eye.

"Pack a suitcase. You're getting out of here," said Agatha.

Toni hauled a suitcase down from the top of a wardrobe and began to stuff clothes into it. Agatha looked round the room. Unlike the rest of the house that she had seen, Toni's room was neat and clean, reminding her bitterly of her own childhood where she had tried to create an island of calm amongst the drunken chaos wrought by her parents.

"He'll kill me if I try to leave," whispered Tony, shutting her suitcase.

"No, he won't. I've got two strong men downstairs who'll make sure he doesn't. Come along."

Agatha stopped at a bank and drew two hundred pounds out of the machine. She paid the two men and dropped them off at the pub before driving Toni to her home.

"Get your bag and come in," ordered Agatha. Carrying the camera case, Agatha led the way.

In the kitchen she ordered Toni to sit down and examined her lip and eye. "You won't need stitches, but you're going to have one hell of a black eye. I'll make you a cup of sweet tea and then check the spare room. I had a guest who's just left, so I'll need to change the sheets."

But when she went upstairs, Agatha found that her excellent cleaner, Doris Simpson, had been in and changed the sheets, cleaned the room and placed a small jug of wild flowers beside the bed.

She returned to the kitchen. "It's all ready. Has this happened before?"

"He's never hit me before. Just played nasty tricks. When I was going to school, if he found my homework, he'd rip it up, things like that."

"Where is your father?"

"I don't know who he is. Ma would never say."

"And your mother drinks a lot?"

"All the time."

"Any others? I mean brothers or sisters?"

"No, just Terry."

"What a mess. I should report all this to the social services. Stay here for a bit until I figure out what to do. Now, have you eaten anything?"

Toni shook her head.

"I'll fix us something, but," said Agatha with a rare burst of honesty, "I'm not the world's best cook."

She searched in the deep freeze and found a packet of lamb stew, given to her the week before by Mrs. Bloxby. She defrosted it and then heated it in the microwave. She put a plate of food in front of Toni and then opened a bottle of wine.

"You're very kind," said Toni awkwardly.

The doorbell rang.

"Does Terry know where I live?" asked Agatha nervously.

"No. I didn't either. You only had phone numbers on that card you gave me."

Agatha went to answer it. Her friend, Sir Charles Fraith, stood on the doorstep.

"Come in," said Agatha. "But I'm in the middle of a bit of a drama."

Charles was as beautifully tailored as ever, his fair hair in an excellent cut and his neat features betraying nothing more than amiable curiosity. Agatha introduced Toni and briefly outlined what had been happening.

Charles helped himself to a glass of wine. "I haven't enough food for you," said Agatha.

"I've just eaten. Do you know what you should do?" said Charles.

"About what?"

"About Toni here."

"It's arranged. She can stay here as long as she wants."

"You'll soon want your own space and start bitching, Agatha."

And Agatha, who had been feeling like a saint for rescuing Toni, glared at him.

"Listen," said Charles. "These days, you can't lose out buying property. Buy her a flat in Mircester and then when she starts earning enough, charge her rent."

Agatha opened her mouth to give an angry retort and then shut it again. Charles might have a point. What if she met the man of her dreams? It wouldn't help to have a pretty young girl in residence.

"I'll think about it," she said gruffly. She saw that Toni had finished eating. "Come along, Toni. I'll take you upstairs.

Have a hot bath and get into bed. You'll feel a lot better after a good night's sleep."

Later, Toni lay in the comfortable bed and looked about her with a kind of wonder. Everything was so clean and cheerful. Chintz curtains fluttered at the open window. Agatha had brought her up a glass of warm milk and two strong painkillers along with magazines and books.

How odd that the terrifying Agatha should turn out to be so motherly. And the cottage with its deep thatched roof was the kind she had seen on chocolate boxes and calendars.

Toni did not expect this heaven to last. But her young life had been full of experience of how to enjoy the moment before the drunken chaos created by her mother and brother descended on her again. She sighed and stretched out and was soon fast asleep.

Toni awoke with a start and looked at the alarm clock beside her bed—and groaned. Nine o'clock! How could she have overslept? She struggled up and saw a note on the bedside table. It was from Agatha. She read: "I think you should take the day off and relax. There is food in the freezer. Help yourself. A."

Toni got up and stretched. Two white fluffy towels had been placed at the end of her bed. She found the bathroom, had a shower and dressed in a blouse, jeans and sandals.

She went into the kitchen. Agatha's cats, Hodge and Boswell, came to meet her. Toni crouched down on the floor and petted them, then stood up and went to the fridge. There were no eggs or bacon. A chest freezer stood against one wall. She lifted the lid. The labels that could still be read showed Agatha's love for microwaveable food such as curries and lasagne.

Toni saw a loaf on the counter and decided to settle for a breakfast of toast and coffee.

She had just finished when the doorbell rang. Toni experienced a pang of fear. What if her brother had come to hunt her down?

There was a spyhole in the door and she peered through it. A pleasant-looking grey-haired woman stood on the step.

Toni opened the door. "I am Mrs. Bloxby," said the woman. "Mrs. Raisin called me. She had not told you how to set the burglar alarm. Let me show you."

"That is kind of you," said Toni. She listened carefully to the instructions. When Mrs. Bloxby had finished, she said, "I also wondered whether you might like to come with me to the vicarage? You must be hungry. Mrs. Raisin only has black coffee and cigarettes for breakfast."

Toni was still hungry so she agreed, and ten minutes later was sitting in the vicarage garden listening to the domestic sounds from the kitchen as Mrs. Bloxby prepared her breakfast.

The sun shone down in all its hazy autumn beauty. From the fields above the village came the sound of a tractor.

The vicar's wife came out with a tray and unloaded a plate of bacon, sausage and eggs, coffee, toast and marmalade.

"This is very good of you," said Toni awkwardly. "Did Mrs. Raisin tell you why I am staying with her?"

"Mrs. Raisin said that you had some trouble at home, that is all."

Silence fell as Toni ate steadily. Mrs. Bloxby took out some knitting. The needles flashed in the sunlight.

Toni finished her meal and sat back with a sigh. "I'll need to find somewhere to live," she said. "I can't stay with Mrs. Raisin forever. We call her Agatha at the office."

Mrs. Bloxby smiled. "It is a very old-fashioned tradition in the village to use second names. I gather you don't want to go home again."

"It's difficult," said Toni. Mrs. Bloxby smiled and continued to knit. "It's like this," said Toni, and then it all burst out of her, all the family troubles.

"What about your father?" asked Mrs. Bloxby.

"I don't know who he is," mumbled Toni.

"I really wouldn't worry about your future," said Mrs. Bloxby. "Mrs. Raisin is a great organizer." She put down her knitting. "Now, I must go about my parish duties."

"Can I help?"

"As a matter of fact, you can. One of my duties is to read to old Mrs. Wilson. She is going blind."

"I can do that."

"I will take you there."

Such as Agatha and Mrs. Bloxby seemed old to the youthful Toni, but Mrs. Wilson seemed as old as an Egyptian mummy. Despite the heat of the day, she was wrapped in shawls. Her face was criss-crossed with deep wrinkles and her scalp showed through her thin grey hair. Mrs. Bloxby introduced Toni and left. Mrs. Wilson turned milky eyes on Toni. "That book there," she ordered. "Begin at the beginning."

Toni picked it up. *A Christmas Carol* by Charles Dickens.

She began to read, reflecting that it was a good thing the old lady still had her hearing and she didn't have to shout. She had never been much of a reader, but she became so involved in the story that she only realized after an hour that Mrs. Wilson had fallen asleep.

Toni put the book down and let herself out. Mrs. Wilson's cottage was at the top of the village. Toni walked down under a green arch of trees and called in at the general stores to ask for directions to Agatha's house because she had forgotten the road. The villagers in the shop were obviously trying not to stare too hard at her black eye.

In the afternoon, Patrick returned. He said that the locals hadn't been very forthcoming at first, until he had stood them a round of drinks. It was then they had begun to talk. "They're really bitter," he said. "Turns out that Mrs. Tamworthy's got building permission for some of her land. It's agricultural land, so they feel she must have bribed someone. They say when she sells, the new owner can put up houses and they'll be expensive houses that no one in the village can afford. They are planning a protest march to the council offices. The ringleader appears to be the publican, called Paul Chambers. He says that Mrs. Tamworthy would be better off dead. He says none of her family would sell the place."

Phil came into the office. "I didn't get very far with Jimmy Tamworthy, but he's a quiet, gentlemanly type. I got the idea that he might consider working in a shop beneath him."

"I don't suppose we can do much more until I get out there for the weekend," said Agatha. "Let's get back to the more mundane cases."

Toni was just wondering whether she should go back to the general stores and perhaps buy something to prepare a dinner for the evening when she heard a key turning in the lock. Agatha must be home early. "I'm in the kitchen," she called.

Charles Fraith walked in. "Have you come to stay?" asked Toni. "I mean, Agatha has only one spare bedroom."

"I may sleep on the sofa or I may go home. It doesn't matter. You still look as if you've been in the wars. Do you have a car?"

"No, I'm seventeen, but I'll be eighteen in two months' time."

"Like a driving lesson?"

Toni's eyes shone. "I'd love that."

When she was with Agatha or Charles, Toni spoke in carefully precise English, unlike the voice she used at home or with her friends. She could hear inside her head, as she spoke, that other, coarser accent struggling to get out.

Charles proved to be a good and patient teacher. He took her up onto the quiet backcountry roads.

By the time they got back to Agatha's cottage, Charles said, "You're a good pupil. You'll be driving in no time at all."

Agatha had arrived home. She looked up as they both came into the kitchen. Toni's eyes were shining and Charles looked amused.

"What have you been up to?" asked Agatha.

"I've been giving Toni driving lessons."

"Good for you. Sit down, Toni. I've got your contract. Read it carefully and sign it at the places I've marked with a cross. Charles, Roy was going to come with me on Saturday to Mrs. Tamworthy's birthday party."

"Who's Mrs. Tamworthy?"

Agatha told him. When she had finished, Charles said, "It all sounds very odd. I'm curious. I'll come with you."

"Thanks. I think the old lady might just be bonkers, but I wasn't going to enjoy being on my own."

"I've finished," said Toni. "It's a generous wage."

"You'll not only be earning it," said Agatha, "you'll soon be paying me rent, so you'll need it. I'm buying a little flat round the corner from the office. You should be able to move in after a fortnight." She raised a hand to cut off a volley of excited thanks from Toni. "As I said, you'll be earning it. Charles, are you staying?"

"May as well. I'll sleep on the sofa."

"You've got a perfectly good bedroom in that mansion of yours," Agatha pointed out, "and it's only half an hour's drive away."

"My aunt is having friends round this evening." Charles lived with his aunt. "It'll be like a geriatric convention. Much more fun here. Tell you what, I'll take you both out for dinner."

"I haven't the right clothes to wear," said Toni, imagining a grand restaurant.

"You'll do as you are," said Agatha. "I'll bet dear Charles here means to take us to the pub."

"You are so right, Aggie."

"Got your wallet?"

"Don't be nasty."

Toni loved the Red Lion with its oak beams, stone floor and little mullioned windows. Agatha was chatting to Charles about the forthcoming weekend. Toni studied her uneasily. She was very grateful to Agatha for all her generosity but was frightened it was merely a whim and Agatha would soon grow tired of playing the Lady Bountiful, not knowing that a good part of Agatha's generosity was prompted by shrewd business acumen. Agatha saw a promising detective, a young detective who would not leave her to go to university as Harry had done. Charles was also a puzzle. He was light and amusing, but she wondered what he really thought about things, not knowing that Agatha, who had known him a long time, often worried about the same thing.

They all ate ham, egg and chips. Agatha and Charles had a glass of wine each and Toni had an orange juice.

When they got back to the cottage, Toni suddenly felt awkward. Were Charles and Agatha having an affair? Charles seemed a bit younger than Agatha. Agatha, despite her stocky figure and small eyes, exuded an air of sexiness of which she seemed totally unaware.

Toni decided to plead an early night. "Have you a copy of *A Christmas Carol*?" she asked.

"Don't think so."

"It's just that your friend, Mrs. Bloxby, came round. She got me to read to this old lady and that was the book. I keep wondering what happens."

Charles laughed. "You've led a charmed life if you don't know. There have been so many films and plays based on that book."

"Never mind," said Agatha. "There's a box of detective stories in the kitchen. Help yourself."

Toni selected a copy of *The Franchise Affair* by Josephine

Tey. It was the first detective story she had ever read. She read on into the night, until her eyelids drooped and she fell asleep.

In the next two days, Agatha found she was engaged to find evidence in two more divorce cases. Toni, who had returned to work the previous day, had done well retrieving two cats and one dog, having taken Mrs. Freedman's advice and gone to the animal shelter.

Agatha turned to her. "I think I'll put you on the Horrington case, Toni," she said. "Here is the file. Study it. It's quite simple. Mrs. Horrington thinks her husband is playing around and wants proof. Phil will give you the camera and lens. You haven't seen your new flat yet. We'll go along after work and you can actually move in tomorrow. I'm paying rent for it until the sale goes through."

Toni was worried. Agatha was paying her a good salary. Agatha had found her a flat. She felt the weight of gratitude and obligation. She hoped against hope she would prove lucky with this divorce case.

Mr. Horrington worked as sales director of a shoe company out on the industrial estate. Toni cycled out to the estate. The day was still sunny and the radio that morning had announced a hosepipe ban.

Her heart sank as she cycled around the industrial estate. The ground around the shoe factory was bare of bushes and trees. Nowhere to hide. How had the others managed to watch him? If he left in his car, she could hardly keep up with him on her bicycle because, unlike at the centre of town, the roads around the industrial estate did not carry much traffic.

She took out her notes and found his home address and headed there instead. Mrs. Horrington opened the door and scowled at the young girl with the fading black eye. "Go away. I'm not buying anything," she said.

She was a carefully preserved woman with expensively blonded hair. Her make-up was quite thick and her lipstick a scarlet slash across her mouth.

"I'm from the agency," said Toni. "I am working on your divorce."

"This is an outrage," exclaimed Mrs. Horrington. "Wait there!"

She marched indoors and Toni waited.

At last the door opened again and a mollified Mrs. Horrington said, "You'd better come in. Mrs. Raisin says you are not only brilliant but lucky. I'll go along with it for the moment."

"I wanted to know if your husband had a favourite restaurant for lunch," said Toni.

"I believe he goes to La Nouvelle Cuisine," she said. "Why?"

"I wondered if he might take someone there."

Mrs. Horrington gave a contemptuous laugh. "He would hardly parade anyone in front of the business community. They all lunch there."

"How did you guess he was having an affair?"

"New underwear. Smells of scent. Looks guilty as hell."

"Have you challenged him?"

"Oh, yes. He said it was all nonsense. He said he would take me on a cruise for a second honeymoon. No sign of him booking anything."

"Do you have a photograph of him? I couldn't find one in the file."

"I gave one to that Raisin woman. Oh, wait here."

After a few minutes, Mrs. Horrington came back with a photograph. It showed a plump middle-aged man with thinning grey hair and a paunch.

"He's dyed his hair black since that was taken," said Mrs. Horrington. "Another sign."

"I'll get back to you," said Toni.

"You'd better do it quick. If you don't have any results by the weekend, I'm employing another agency."

Toni peddled under the unseasonally hot sun into the centre of Mircester. She propped her bike outside the restaurant and went in, the camera slung round her neck.

A pleasant wave of air conditioning hit her. A formidable maître d' approached. "I am taking pictures for a new magazine called *Gloucester Food*," said Toni, trying to imitate Charles's polished vowels as best as she could.

"I don't know that my customers would like having their meals interrupted by photographs," said the maître d'.

Toni noticed there was a service hatch from the kitchen. "I could shoot a few photographs through that service hatch," she said. "I'll be very discreet. It's best to take photographs when the restaurant is as busy as this."

The maître d' hesitated only a moment. Although the lunch hour was still busy, attendance in the evenings had been falling off. The restaurant could do with the publicity.

"Just for a little while," he said. "We don't use the service hatch any more. The waiters carry the food straight in from the kitchen."

He led Toni into the kitchen. She raised the service hatch and then stood back. She wanted anyone looking over to get

47

used to seeing it open. She studied the photograph of Mr. Horrington and then cautiously approached the service hatch and looked through.

She saw Mr. Horrington just getting to his feet and helping a comparatively young woman into her jacket.

Toni darted out of the kitchen and said to the startled maître d', "I've left some equipment outside."

She positioned herself outside the restaurant. There would not be much point photographing the pair if they stood apart and showed no signs of affection. Mr. Horrington could just claim it was a buyer.

He emerged with the woman. Toni raised the camera. He whispered something in her ear and she giggled. Toni snapped a picture, glad the sound of the shutter was drowned by the traffic. Then Mr. Horrington looked hurriedly up and down the street, not seeing Toni, who had crouched down behind a parked car. Toni rose to her feet again just to witness Mr. Horrington and the woman engaged in a steamy kiss.

"Gotcha!" she muttered, clicking the camera and taking as many photographs as she could.

Later, Agatha said, amazed, "You *are* lucky. I've followed him for days. Damn it. I concentrated on the evenings. He always seemed to be working late."

"Then she probably works at the shoe factory as well," said Toni.

"Good. I'll go and see Mrs. Horrington. Do you want to come with me?"

"No, I'll leave it to you."

"Had lunch?"

"Not yet."

"Go out and get something and we'll go to that flat when I get back."

When Agatha had gone, Toni asked Mrs. Freedman, "When do I get my pay? I'm running low."

"On Friday. I gather you don't have a bank account so you will be paid cash until you set one up. But you haven't yet claimed any expenses. I can give you some money out of the petty cash for just now. Take an expenses sheet with you and fill it in. You can put down for lunch at that posh restaurant."

"I don't have a receipt."

"We'll assume you lost it. Here's forty pounds for the moment."

Toni was determined to keep as much of the money as possible, so she went to the nearest Burger King. She was just finishing a burger when she looked through the window and saw her brother, Terry, lurching along the street. He looked drunk. She bent down and hid until he had passed.

Later that afternoon, Agatha took her to see the flat. It was very small: one tiny living room, a small bedroom, a minuscule kitchen and a bathroom. The bathroom was surprisingly the largest room in the place.

"I'm buying the furnishings as well," said Agatha. "They're pretty horrible, but you can change them as you go along. You've got a bed at least and I put bedclothes on it and some towels in the bathroom. Now I'll take you home and you can collect your bag. Everything went through quickly and so instead of waiting a fortnight, you can move in right away."

Toni was choked up with gratitude as Agatha handed her the keys. She had an impulse to hug her but reflected that one probably didn't hug such as the formidable Agatha Raisin.

Agatha, as she drove towards Carsely, was prey to mixed feelings. It was all right to think that Toni was just lucky, but she herself should have thought of that restaurant. Toni's black eye was fading fast. How wonderful to be young again, thought Agatha. How marvellous not to suffer the indignities of approaching old age: spreading waistline, moustache, hair dye and aching hip. She resolved to go back to the beautician's, Beau Monde, in Evesham and get Dawn to work her magic on her face before the weekend.

The weekend! It all seemed a rather silly waste of time the more she thought of it.

FOUR

†

AGATHA SET out with Charles for the Manor House on Saturday morning feeling low in spirits.

"What's up with you?" asked Charles. "You've gone all moody."

"It's these divorce cases. I hate them. The two that Toni wrapped up weren't too bad."

"Why?"

"No children involved. But there are in the two new ones."

"Not developing a conscience at this late time in life, Aggie?"

"I am not late in life, but yes, it does seem dirty."

"You can't avoid divorce cases if you're going to run a detective agency."

"It's not only that," said Agatha, "it's this weekend. I've been lost in dreams of a Poirot-type set-up and I feel now it's just the paranoia of one batty old woman."

"We'll suffer today," said Charles, "and if we decide she really is bonkers, we'll clear off. But from what you've told me, she certainly seems to have thought up a will to make herself a prime target."

"You've got the map," said Agatha, who was driving. "Remember to direct me to the entrance from Upper Tapor. I don't want to have to endure that long walk across the fields again. Besides, it looks like rain."

"Occasionally it's looked like rain in the past few days," said Charles, "but the clouds then disappear and the sun blazes down again. Cheer up. You'll feel better once we're there and suss things out. Then if the old girl is still alive by this evening, we could push off."

"I have to stay. She's paying me handsomely by the day and now that I'm paying Toni full detective wages, I need the money."

"Your generosity surprises me sometimes, Aggie."

"Coming from someone who always forgets to find his wallet when we're out for dinner, you should not be surprised at all."

"Miaow!"

Just outside Upper Tapor, they saw a sign, MANOR HOUSE. Agatha drove along a well-kept drive and soon they found themselves at the house.

Phyllis Tamworthy greeted them. "I thought you were bringing your son," she said to Agatha.

"Roy Silver is not my son," said Agatha crossly. "This is a colleague of mine, Sir Charles Fraith."

"A 'sir'?" Phyllis grinned. "My snobby daughters are going to love you. I'll show you to your rooms—or are you sleeping together?"

"No," said Agatha, ignoring a whispered, mocking "Maybe" from Charles.

Agatha found her bedroom a surprise. Obviously Phyllis had decided to forgo the appearance of a stately mansion on the upper floors. Everything looked as if it had come from Ikea. Also, it was decorated in shades of brown: dark brown carpet, lighter brown curtains, mid-brown painted walls and a rust-coloured duvet on the bed.

There was a television set on a table by the window. Agatha reflected that it looked exactly like a bedroom in a three-star hotel.

Charles came in as she was unpacking. "I'm not a romantic like you," he said, "but I must admit the bedrooms come as a surprise. Hardly the right sinister setting. This house depresses me. It must have once been a charming family home."

Phyllis came in without knocking, drying her hands on her apron. "They'll all be in the drawing room just after one o'clock. Jimmy closes the shop half day on Saturday. Stupid. It should be his busiest day, but there's no arguing with him. When you're ready, come down."

When she had left, Agatha said, "You unpacked quickly."

"Didn't unpack at all," said Charles laconically. "Took one look at the bedroom and decided a quick getaway might be a good idea. Let's go down and face the music."

On entering the drawing room, Agatha surveyed the assembled company and decided with a sinking heart that she had never seen a bunch of such ordinary people before.

As Phyllis introduced them, Agatha took mental notes so that she would remember who was who. Daughter Sadie, married to Sir Henry Field, was small and dumpy, and dressed in a bright blue silk trouser suit. Sir Henry was so bland and pompous that there was something not quite real about him, as if he had come from Central Casting. Divorced daughter Fran was as thin as her sister was fat, with tightly permed white hair, indeterminate features as if someone had taken a sponge and tried to erase her face, and wearing a baggy tweed skirt and Aertex blouse. I haven't seen an Aertex blouse in years, thought Agatha.

Son Bert was small and red-faced, bald and with pursed-up lips, as if perpetually discontented. He was wearing a suit that had obviously been tailored for him when he was a slimmer man.

His wife, Alison, was a domineering woman in tweeds. She had a heavy truculent face and slightly protruding brown eyes. Fran's daughter, Annabelle, made Charles's eyes light up. She was in her late forties with thick auburn hair and creamy skin. She stood out in the pedestrian-looking crowd. Sadie's daughter, Lucy, on the other hand, looked as dreary as her mother, and her eight-year-old daughter, Jennifer, had "spoilt brat" written all over her.

Agatha had phoned Phyllis the night before to ask her where she should say they had met, and Phyllis told her to say they had met five years ago in Bournemouth when she, Phyllis, had been on holiday at the Imperial Hotel.

Jimmy, the favourite, was last to arrive. His shoulders were stooped. He had a long face and a beaten air, as if years of working at a job he hated had bowed him down.

Agatha wondered if Phyllis planned to cater for and serve

the lot of them lunch. Sherry was served. Even to Agatha's un-educated palate, it tasted awful. Charles muttered he thought it was British sherry, and so it turned out. "Do you remember the days when you could buy British sherry?" said Phyllis. "It was so cheap that every time I had an empty bottle, I would go down to the off-licence and get it filled up. It was on draught. I've still got bottles of it in the cellar."

"Oh, Mother," wailed Fran, casting an anxious look at Charles. "What will Sir Charles think of you?"

They were summoned to the large dining room. Two women, who looked as if they came from the village from their appear-ance, and from their behaviour as if they were part of the protest group, served the first course of ham-and-pea soup, slopping the soup into plates, and scowling all around.

The long mahogany table shone and the china was of the finest, but placed strategically down the table were bottles of HP sauce and bottles of ketchup.

The second course was steak and kidney pie with chips and peas. The meat was tough and there was more kidney than steak and the pastry was like a wet book. Phyllis's choice of wine was served. Blue Nun.

"I'm out of here—fast," whispered Charles, who was seated next to Agatha.

"Don't leave me," pleaded Agatha.

Conversation was stilted. They talked among themselves about the weather and about people Agatha did not know.

Over the apple pie and custard—sour apples and lumpy custard—Phyllis, flushed with several glasses of Blue Nun, asked, "When do I get my presents?"

"We all agreed we would give you your presents when the brandy and coffee is served."

"If you mean the end of the meal, fine," said Phyllis. "But you know I don't like brandy. You're all going to have some of my elderberry wine. Agatha," she shouted down the table, "I pick my own elderberries and make my own wine. Nothing like it."

"I'll bet," muttered Charles gloomily.

As the coffee was served, one by one the family rose and went out, returning with their presents. Not one of them, it seemed, had thought it necessary to loosen the purse strings to buy the old woman a decent present. Several gave books that Agatha recognized as ones currently on sale in the sort of bookshops specializing in remainders. Jimmy gave his mother a hot water bag in the shape of a teddy bear. Fran gave her a necklace. Agatha had seen one just like it recently in the jewellery section of Marks & Spencer.

Sadie stared at Agatha and Charles. "Haven't you brought Mother a present?"

"Hadn't time to drop into the thrift shop," whispered Charles.

Agatha could feel laughter bubbling up inside her. She tried to suppress it but up it came and she laughed and laughed.

Phyllis's voice cut across the laughter. "I didn't tell Agatha it was my birthday," she said.

Agatha recovered, mopped her eyes and apologized while they all looked at her suspiciously.

Then just as they were all, with the exception of Phyllis, grimacing over their elderberry wine, eight-year-old Jennifer piped up. "My gran," she said, meaning Sadie, "says it's not worth giving you anything good cos you're out to screw the lot of us."

There was a shocked silence. Then Jennifer's mother,

Lucy, said, "The dear child was only joking. It's that dreadful comprehensive school she goes to. If she went to a private school, she wouldn't speak like that."

Phyllis rose to her feet. "I'm tired," she announced. "We will meet at six o'clock for high tea."

"Oh, *Mother,*" groaned Sadie. "No one, but no one, has high tea any more."

"I do," said Phyllis firmly.

"Wanna go home!" screamed Jennifer.

"A very good idea, darling," said her mother, Lucy. Jennifer's grandmother, Sadie, chimed in, "Yes, do go, my darlings. She's not going to leave us anything no matter how long we stay here."

"Good idea," echoed Annabelle. "I'm leaving as well."

"Come on," Charles said to Agatha, "let's go for a walk."

Outside, Charles looked at the sky. "I think the Indian summer's finally coming to an end. What an awful lunch."

"You mean dinner," Agatha corrected him. "At least with Annabelle, Lucy and the horrible child gone, it leaves fewer people to watch. That leaves Sadie, Sir Henry, Fran, Bert, Jimmy and Alison. And I can't see one of them as a potential murderer."

"Let's suffer it all until tomorrow. Or do you want to leave now?"

"Phyllis is paying me for the whole weekend. Don't abandon me, Charles."

"Of course not," said Charles, who was already planning to get a friend to phone him with some urgent news that would give him an excuse to leave.

"I think they all might still be in the dining room," said Agatha. "It might be a good idea to listen. That's the dining room over there. I can see Sir Henry pacing up and down and waving his arms. The windows are open. If we stroll nearer and stand behind those laurel bushes, we should be able to hear everything."

They made their way cautiously forward until they were screened by the bushes. Sir Henry's well articulated voice reached their ears. "I have tried to reason with her. Cutting off her own flesh and blood."

Bert said, "What about you pleading with her, Jimmy? You were always her favourite."

Jimmy's voice reached Agatha and Charles, loaded with venom. "Favourite?" he spat out. "Chained to that bloody shop. How are your bunions this morning, Mrs. Smith? Pah! And now they all hate me because she's selling up here. I'll soon be in debt. I asked her to help me out and she said it was up to me to run a successful business."

Sadie chimed in. "I happen to know she's changing something in her will."

There was a startled silence.

"She told me," said Sadie. "She enjoyed telling me. She's going to alter it next week. She said she'd been on the phone to her solicitor the day before she spoke to me. She's going to leave it all to build a technical college in Daddy's name. She's going to start the building of it as soon as she sells this place, and if she dies, she's making sure the building goes on. And she's leaving the college to the state, so we can't even sell it."

Alison, Bert's wife, snarled, "If only she would drop dead."

"I'm going for a lie-down," said Sadie. "Oh, Miss Crampton, yes, you can clear the table now."

There came a scraping back of chairs. Charles and Agatha moved away.

"Gosh and double gosh," said Agatha. "They sound murderous."

"They sound like a lot of bores," said Charles. "Relax. Nothing's going to happen."

"You're right. I'll get the dreadful high tea over with and clear off in the morning. Will you be free for Christmas dinner?"

"Aggie, it's October."

"I know, but I am going to have a really splendid old-fashioned Christmas."

"Your last Christmas dinner was a disaster. What's with you and Christmas?"

"I want to have one Christmas the way it's supposed to be."

"It never is, Aggie. Grow up. People are under stress. They drink too much, they fight, they decide they've always hated each other. You're a romantic."

"And what's up with that? It's all sex, sex, sex these days."

"Love usually comes along disguised as lust or because of delayed gratification like *Brave New World*."

"I'll show you," said Agatha. "Just turn up for my Christmas dinner, that's all."

"Aha, there's more to this than meets the eye. Where's James?"

"Travelling. But I'm sure he'll be home for Christmas."

"And standing under the mistletoe?"

"I'm going in," said Agatha crossly. "Oh, was that a spot of rain?"

Charles looked up at the sky. "Feels like it."

"I thought the weather would break with a magnificent thunderstorm," said Agatha.

"And Phyllis would slump dead over the dining table to crashes of thunder, her dead face lit by flashes of lightning?"

Agatha gave a reluctant laugh. "Something like that."

"Stop writing scripts. Life is so often boring and predictable."

A sullen company shuffled back into the dining room at six o'clock. Outside the windows, rain was falling steadily. They took their places as ordered by Phyllis, who took her customary place at the head of the table. Apart from Agatha and Charles, the remainder consisting of Sadie, Fran, Sir Henry, Bert, Alison and Jimmy slumped into their chairs. High tea was already laid out. An urn with cups, milk and sugar stood on the sideboard. A large cake stand in the centre of the table held thin slices of white buttered bread on the bottom layer, teacakes on the second, scones on the third and ersatz-cream cakes on the top.

In front of each person was a plate containing two thin slices of shiny ham, peas, chips, as well as a bowl of peculiar-looking salad.

Agatha poked at the salad with her fork. "What's in this?"

"My own creation," said Phyllis proudly. "Parsley, grated parsnip, grated carrot, grated turnip and lettuce. Have the others gone home?"

"Yes, Mother," said Jimmy. His face in the grey light from the rain-washed windows looked pale.

"Their loss," said Phyllis. "Dig in. I've sent the village women home. No use paying people to serve you when you can serve yourselves."

Phyllis made several attempts at conversation but no one replied. Agatha, unable to bear the following silence, started talking about the weather, saying that although the gardens needed the rain, it was all very depressing. Her voice trailed off as no one seemed to be paying attention.

After another long silence, Fran suddenly picked up her bowl of salad and threw it into the empty fireplace. "Sod you, Mother, and your bloody rabbit food and your cheap ways. You're about to disinherit your own flesh and blood!" She burst into tears and ran from the table.

To Agatha's surprise, Phyllis's eyes gleamed with amusement. "You asked for that," said Bert.

"We'd better get out and find a pub this evening," muttered Charles to Agatha. "I can't eat any of this muck."

Jimmy half-rose from the table. "Mother, I want to sell the shop!"

"It's in my name, son. You'll get the title deeds when I'm dead."

In a bitter little voice, Jimmy said, "And when will that be?"

Phyllis looked shocked and hurt for the first time since Agatha had met her.

She rose to her feet and stumbled. An odd expression crossed her face. She tried to take a step and fell over on the floor. Jimmy rushed to help her to her feet.

"I'm tired, that's all," said Phyllis. "Help me to my room."

She staggered as if she was drunk as her son supported her out of the dining room.

"I think you'd better call a doctor," said Agatha.

"She's had turns before," said Bert. "She's got a weak heart. She always comes around if she gets a rest."

"I still think you should call her doctor," insisted Agatha. "Give me his name and I'll call him."

"You are not family," said Bert crossly. "There's no need to make a fuss."

Upstairs afterwards, Charles joined Agatha in her room. "I went along to see how Phyllis was doing. Fran was coming out of her room. She said she was fine, so no poisoning. I mean if she had been poisoned, there would have been vomiting or convulsions. Let's get out of here for a couple of hours and find a pub."

"Not the local. Somewhere else," said Agatha.

Feeling much restored after a pub dinner of sausage, egg and chips, Agatha and Charles returned to the manor. "Lead me to Phyllis's room," said Agatha. The sounds of television coming from the drawing room reached their ears. "They're all probably downstairs watching the box."

"Follow me," said Charles.

He led the way upstairs and along a corridor. "It's been done up like a hotel," he said. "The big bedrooms seem to have been split in two. Here we are." He rapped gently on the door.

No reply.

"Go on in," urged Agatha.

Charles turned the handle and they both walked in. By the light of a bedside lamp they could see Phyllis.

Agatha walked forward and looked down at her. "Charles," she said shakily, "I think she's dead."

Phyllis was lying on top of the bedclothes dressed in what she had been wearing for high tea. Bits of salad stuck to her black top.

Charles felt for a pulse and found none.

Fran's voice sounded from the doorway, "What are you doing?"

"I think your mother's dead," said Agatha.

Fran rushed up to the bed. She stared at her mother for a brief moment and then reached to pick up the bedside phone.

"Let's leave the room as it is," commanded Agatha. "Phone from downstairs."

"What . . . ?"

"I think your mother may have been murdered."

"You're stark staring mad. I will phone the doctor and you'll find it was a heart attack."

"I am not a friend of your mother," said Agatha. "I am a detective. She invited me here because she told me she suspected a family member would kill her."

Fran turned paper-white. Agatha registered that the news that she was a detective and that Phyllis had suspected one of her family might murder her had shocked Fran more than the death of her mother.

"It's all madness," whispered Fran. "I'll phone from downstairs."

"Let's leave and lock the door. We'll wait for the police."

The news spread throughout the house and they all gathered in the drawing room.

"Dr. Huxley is on his way," said Fran.

"Didn't you call the police?" demanded Agatha.

There came a shocked chorus of "whys?"

"Because," said Agatha loudly above the babble, "as I told Fran, I am a detective hired by your mother to protect her this weekend. She thought one of you might try to kill her."

"She was old," said Sir Henry. "Losing her marbles. There's proof of it. Here's the doctor now."

Agatha quickly scanned the faces around the room. They betrayed various levels of shock and apprehension but not one of them was grieving.

Bert went to the door and ushered the doctor in. "Here's the key to her room," said Agatha. "I thought it better to lock it until the police get here."

Dr. Huxley was a small, thin, fussy man. He took the key from her and said firmly, "I am sure I will find that Mrs. Tamworthy died of a heart attack. Her heart was not strong. She was taking heart medicine."

Bert led the doctor upstairs.

"I'm going out for some air," said Agatha.

"It's pouring," said Charles.

"Don't care."

Agatha went outside and pulled out her mobile phone and called Mircester police and spoke rapidly.

Then she hurried back inside.

"As soon as the doctor leaves," said Sadie to Agatha, "you can jolly well pack your bags and leave. This is our house now and you are not welcome."

Silence fell as they all waited.

After what seemed an age, the doctor came down the stairs. "Mrs. Tamworthy died peacefully in her sleep when her heart stopped. I have signed the death certificate and given it to Mr. Albert Tamworthy."

Fran turned glittering eyes on Agatha. "You see? Now, get out."

Agatha heard police sirens in the distance and said, "I've called the police."

There came outraged cries all round. Then Fran flew at Agatha in a rage. Agatha dived behind an armchair. Fran reached over it and seized her by the hair. Charles dragged her off.

"You have no right to question my judgement," said the doctor when the protests and shouts had died down.

The sirens wailed their way up the drive.

Then there came a loud knocking at the front door and a cry of "Police!"

Bert went to answer it. Detective Inspector Wilkes came in, followed by Detective Sergeant Bill Wong. Bill was a friend of Agatha's. Behind them came four police constables.

"I am Dr. Huxley," he said. "I have examined Mrs. Tamworthy and signed the death certificate."

Wilkes ignored him. "Mrs. Raisin? When you phoned, you said something about a letter?"

Agatha produced it from her handbag. Wilkes put on a pair of latex gloves, read it quickly and then handed it to Bill, who donned gloves as well before carefully putting it in an envelope.

"In view of this letter," said Wilkes, "we will need to wait for the police pathologist, who is on his way here. I will wait for his report."

"If the dining room hasn't been cleared," said Agatha, "it might be an idea to lock it up for the moment. Her death could have been caused by something Mrs. Tamworthy ate."

"Show one of the police officers the dining room," ordered Wilkes. He heard the sound of a car arriving and looked out of the window. "The pathologist has arrived. A forensic team will be here shortly. Do not leave this room, any of you."

A constable let the pathologist in and Wilkes and Bill followed him up the stairs.

Everyone sat as if turned to stone.

Then Wilkes called to a constable, who went upstairs. He soon clattered back down and went out to the pathologist's car and came back in carrying a heavy case and went upstairs again. Agatha, who had risen to watch from the window, wondered what was going on.

Jimmy suddenly lit up a cigarette. After some hesitation, so did Sadie. With a little sigh of relief, Agatha found her own packet of cigarettes.

The clock on the mantelpiece gave a preliminary whirr before chiming out the hour. Eleven o'clock.

Just as it seemed as if they would have to wait all night, Wilkes came in. "The pathologist has conducted a preliminary examination with a portable desorption electrospray ionization mass spectrometer."

"So? Stop baffling us with science and get on with it," said Sir Henry.

"From the condition of the body, combined with the scraps of salad on her dress and a plant root clutched in one hand, he has come to the conclusion that Mrs. Tamworthy was poisoned with some alkaloid plant such as hemlock. You will continue to remain here while the forensic team conduct a search of the house. A mobile police unit has arrived and is outside of the house. I will summon you for questioning, one at a time. You first, Mrs. Raisin. Follow me."

White, stricken faces watched as Agatha followed Wilkes from the room.

Charles stifled a yawn. He was suddenly bored. He wondered how soon he could leave.

*   *   *

In the police unit, Wilkes faced Agatha. "Begin at the beginning," he said.

Agatha told him again about the letter and then about the will and the threat to leave the money in the will to the founding of a technical college. She then told him about Phyllis's plan to sell the house and estate also to fund the college and how the villagers were riled up.

Wilkes then asked her what they had eaten. "We had individual bowls of salad," said Agatha. "Maybe someone prepared a special bowl for Mrs. Tamworthy. When she rose from the dining table, it was as if she was drunk. She could hardly walk. Does it cause a form of paralysis?"

"I gather from the pathologist," said Wilkes, "that a strong dose of poison hemlock would gradually paralyse the whole body. Her mind would remain acute until the end. There was no bell beside the bed and no way of summoning help."

"Couldn't she shout?"

"No, her vocal cords would be paralysed. A smaller dose and she might have had fever and vomiting to alert someone."

"It was a grated salad," said Agatha.

"The root of poison hemlock looks a good bit like parsnip," said Wilkes. "Have you any idea, Mrs. Raisin, which one of them might have committed the murder?"

"At the moment, I think it's possible all of them might be able to have done it. Charles and I went to the pub for a meal, but before we went Fran was coming out of Mrs. Tamworthy's room. She said she looked all right. Oh, and Fran was furious about being disinherited—well, not exactly disinherited, but Phyllis planned to build a technical college using the money from the sale of the estate and leave the college to the state—and chucked her bowl of salad into the fireplace. Then, two women from the village served dinner. Dinner was in the middle of the day. Mind you, I think they went off after they had cleared up. Mrs. Tamworthy seemed proud that she had created the salads herself. And where did she get the plant root? I swear there was nothing in her hands when she left the dining room."

"And daughter Sadie's family left after lunch?"

"Yes, and Annabelle, as well." Agatha hesitated. She wondered whether to tell Wilkes about listening at the window but decided against it. She was aware of Bill Wong, her friend, watching her impassively.

"That will be all for now," said Wilkes, "but I may want to talk to you later." He turned to a waiting constable. "Tell Sir Charles Fraith to step over."

Agatha got hurriedly to her feet. She must warn Charles not to say anything about listening at the window.

But Wilkes said, "Just a moment. I noticed none of them seemed particularly grief-stricken. There's not a chance they could all have been in it together?"

"I don't know," said Agatha.

"Remember, anything you hear or find out, you must tell me."

"Yes, yes." Agatha hurried out to find Charles being ushered in by the constable.

"A word, Charles," she said.

"Later," said Charles and walked on into the mobile police unit.

A change had taken over the family when Agatha returned to the drawing room. Sadie, Sir Henry, Fran, Bert, Alison and Jimmy were all registering grief for the first time.

"Poor mother!" wailed Fran as soon as she saw Agatha and put a handkerchief up to her suspiciously dry eyes. Sadie was genuinely crying, as was Jimmy. Bert looked white and strained, as did his wife. Sir Henry was pacing up and down, muttering, "Terrible, terrible."

"It must have been one of those villagers," said Alison. "They've been holding meetings and plotting for ages. Anyone can just walk into the kitchen by the side door."

"But Mother didn't make up the salads until just before tea," said Fran.

"How do you know that?" asked Agatha.

"I went into the kitchen to try to make her see sense," said Fran. "It's no use you all looking at me like that. I didn't touch the salad."

The wind had gradually been rising and was now howling around the building.

Suddenly the lights went out.

"There are candles in the kitchen," said Fran, "but we're not allowed to leave the room."

"There's an oil lamp over there," said Jimmy. "I'll light it."

There came the scraping sound of a match being lit and then the oil lamp blossomed into light, sending out a golden glow.

"The police van's still lit up," remarked Sir Henry.

"They've got a generator," said Alison.

The door opened and Charles came in, followed by the constable.

"Lady Field," said the constable, "you're next."

"I'll come with her," said Sir Henry.

"My orders were to take only Lady Field," said the constable firmly.

"Come on, Aggie." Charles patted her on the head. "We can go."

"Just like that!"

"Just like that. Come on. Let's go upstairs and pack. Some policewoman's waiting to escort us to make sure we don't poison anyone on the road out."

As soon as they were in the car, Agatha said, "I didn't tell them about listening at the window."

"I did," said Charles.

Agatha wailed, "Now I'll get a rocket!"

"Why didn't you tell them?"

"It seemed so sneaky."

"You're a detective. You're expected to be sneaky. Anyway, Bill's going to call on us in the morning to take a full statement."

FIVE

†

TONI LAY in bed in her little flat and listened to the rain
drumming on the roof. She wondered if her brother or mother
would contact the police. But after some worrying, she
doubted it. Agatha would explain why she had ridden to the
rescue and Terry would be charged. No more lying in bed
with the pillow over her head listening to the loud noise of the
television set downstairs or the occasional screams of her
mother having the DTs in the bedroom next door.

Her gratitude to Agatha weighed down on her like a burden. She hoped a really important case would come her way
and she would solve it. That would be a good way to pay
Agatha back for all she had done.

Agatha drove slowly to her office the next morning through a
rain-washed sunny countryside. Instead of Bill calling on her,

she had received a phone call to tell her to report to police headquarters. The leaves were turning yellow, gold and brown. The pretty Cotswolds looked their best, free at last from the burden of tourists.

The Cotswolds in the middle of England are a beauty spot, a picture-postcard area with thatched cottages and gardens crammed with flowers.

Agatha, not often very sensitive to beauty, nonetheless could not help noticing the splendour of the morning and suddenly wished she were less driven, less ambitious and could retire into the embrace of a quiet domestic country life.

But as she reached the drab outskirts of Mircester, she began to plan the day ahead. She would need to explain why she had not told the police about listening at the window. She would also need to explain why cavalier Charles had suddenly decided to go to his own home, telling her that the police could interview him there.

When she got to the office, Mrs. Freedman told her the police had called and she was to go immediately to Mircester police headquarters to make a statement. Agatha groaned. Facing Bill would have been bad enough, but now she would have to explain herself to his superior.

She noticed Charles's car parked outside the police station. So he had been summoned as well.

She entered the police headquarters. It had recently been refurbished to make it look more "customer friendly." Gone was the institutional green, to be replaced with what was meant to be sunny yellow but was the colour of sulphur. Two plastic palms, their fronds already covered in dust, stood in two pots looming over a shiny imitation-leather sofa and two plastic chairs.

Agatha gave her name to the desk sergeant and was told to wait. And wait she did, longing for a cigarette. It was a full half-hour before she was summoned.

She was led to an interview room, noticing it had escaped the redecoration. The same scarred table with coffee-ring marks and old cigarette burns from the days when smoking was allowed. The same dull green walls.

"Sit down, Mrs. Raisin," said Wilkes. Bill was not there. Instead there was a woman in a grey power suit. Detective Sergeant Collins had a drab, sallow face, brown hair pulled back into a ponytail, a thin mouth and hooded eyes.

She put a tape in the recording machine and announced, "Interview with Mrs. Agatha Raisin commencing. Detective Inspector Wilkes and Detective Sergeant Collins conducting the interview. Time ten-five A.M."

Agatha realized with a sinking heart as the interview began that Collins was going to ask all the questions. She had considered Wilkes severe in times past, but Collins fired questions at her in an aggressive manner and with an accusatory tone.

"Now," snapped Collins at one point, "you listened at the dining room window, according to Sir Charles, and yet you failed to tell the police what you had heard. I have here Sir Charles Fraith's statement. Let me read you a bit."

She read out an accurate report of what they had both heard as they had listened outside the window.

"Would you agree with this?" asked Collins.

"Yes, that is correct."

"So why didn't you tell us? Is there anything else you are hiding from us?"

"No," said Agatha miserably, feeling her face turn red. "I've told you everything."

73

"You consider yourself an experienced detective?" sneered Collins.

Agatha sat silently, glaring at her.

"Very well. We will accept your lame excuse for the moment . . ."

The questioning went on remorselessly for two hours. Feeling as if she had been mugged, Agatha finally emerged blinking in the sunlight, and looked outside the police station. Charles's car was gone.

She told herself she should be used to his erratic behaviour. Agatha made her way to her office. Her small staff were waiting for her to get the day's instructions.

Agatha was about to begin when there was a knock at the office door and then Alison Tamworthy walked in. Despite the sunny day, she was wearing a tweed skirt and cotton blouse under a Barbour. Her normally pugnacious face showed signs of recent crying.

She stared at Agatha. "I don't care what the others say," she said. "I have to know."

"Please sit down," urged Agatha. "You want us to find out who killed your mother-in-law?"

"That's it. The others say, 'Oh, just let it go.' All they think about is the money. But I can't go on wondering and wondering. They don't know it, but suspicion will hang over the lot of them until this is cleared up. I have my own money."

Agatha signalled to Mrs. Freedman, who came forward with a notebook. "I'll need all the names and addresses," said Agatha.

"I can give you that," said Alison. "Jimmy lives above the shop but has moved into the manor and will continue to do so until we decide what to do with the estate. They are all still at the manor. I want you to come back with me. I want to tell them all that I have engaged you."

"Do you think one of them did it?" asked Agatha.

"I can't believe that. I think it must be one of the trouble-makers from the village. Paul Chambers is the ringleader."

"Right," said Agatha. "Mrs. Freedman will draw up a contract for you to sign. Toni, get Mrs. Tamworthy a coffee."

While Mrs. Freedman prepared the contract and Alison sipped coffee, Agatha gave Phil and Patrick their instructions for the day. Toni looked at her dismally. Agatha appeared to have forgotten her existence.

"Right," said Agatha when the contract was signed. "You go ahead to the manor, Mrs. Tamworthy, and break the news to them that you have employed me and I will follow after, say, half an hour."

When Alison had left, Agatha grinned. "Great! Nice to get something different from divorces. Toni, I want you to come with me to see if that famous luck of yours can dig up something."

As Agatha drove towards Lower Tapor, Toni sat in the passenger seat in a state of excitement. She, Toni Gilmour, was going to a manor house! Ideas of grandeur culled from Merchant Ivory films floated through her head. Would there be a butler? Tea on the terrace? Croquet on the lawn? She was wearing a denim blouse and jeans and wished Agatha had let her go home to change into something more suitable.

As they approached the gates, Agatha said, "I want you to study each one of them and give me your impressions. The police will still be there and they won't be happy to see us, but I'm used to that."

As Agatha parked the car, she could see Bill Wong's head

through a window of the mobile police unit. He appeared to be interviewing someone.

Alison met them at the door. "Sir Henry is being interviewed again. The rest are in the drawing room. Come with me."

Jimmy, Bert, Sadie and Fran were slumped in chairs in the drawing room. They all stared angrily at Agatha. Bert said, "I have told my wife that I cannot see what you can do that the police can't. Waste of money."

"It's my money I'm using," snapped Alison.

"Well, we're not going to cooperate," said Fran.

Alison strode to the fireplace and stood facing them with her hands on her hips. "Don't you all see! If this murder isn't solved, it'll hang over our heads forever. People will look at us and say, 'That's the family that murdered their mother.' Say we decide to sell. People will try to drive the price down because of our shameful reputation."

The money bit struck a chord, thought Toni, covertly studying the faces in the room.

There was a long silence. Glances were exchanged. At last Bert said with obvious reluctance, "Oh, go ahead. It shouldn't bother any of us because none of us did it."

"Mrs. Tamworthy . . ." began Agatha.

"Call me Alison."

"Very well. If forensics have finished with the kitchen, I'd like to have a look at it."

"Come with me," said Alison.

Agatha swung round to Toni. "Why don't you sit down for a bit," she ordered the girl. "I'll be back presently."

When she had left, Sadie, Fran, Bert and Jimmy all looked at Toni for a long moment. Then Sadie picked up a magazine and began to read, Jimmy walked to the window and stared out, Fran began to stitch at a tapestry frame and Bert opened a newspaper.

Toni looked around the room. The manor house was not what she had expected. There was no feeling of antiquity. From the outside, it looked like an old building, maybe eighteenth century, made of mellow Cotswold stone. To judge from the drawing room, it looked as if everything old had been ripped out of the house, and an interior designer brought in. The sofa and chairs were chintz-covered and without any sign of comfortable wear. Toni thought it looked like a hotel which had been decorated to look like a manor house.

Her gaze fell on Jimmy. He was standing at the window chewing his fingernails. There was an air of defeat about him. Fran, with her tightly permed hair and discontented face, did not look upper-class. Toni thought that if you put her in a flowered apron, a turban and stuck a cigarette in her mouth, then she would look like one of those northern women in mill towns one saw in old photographs of World War ll.

Bert, too, looked out of place with his red face and bald head. And Sadie, small and dumpy, was of a type that could be seen on any council house estate. Agatha had told her on the drive to Lower Tapor that she was married to a baronet. Odd. Toni, who had expected them all to be like Sir Charles, was disappointed.

Agatha found there was not much to see in the kitchen. Any makings of salad and any utensils that might have been used preparing the high tea had been taken away for analysis.

She turned to Alison. "Do you know how long the police are going to be here?"

"I think their mobile unit will be leaving this afternoon after we have all signed our statements."

"And then what are everyone's plans?"

"We're all going to the lawyer's late this afternoon to make sure the will is still the same. That is, divided amongst us four ways. After that, I don't know. Fran suggested we should all stay together for a few days to decide what to do about the estate. Fran wants to keep it in the family and Sadie would like that as well. But Jimmy wants to sell the place and so does Bert."

"You see," said Agatha, "I can't get much further while the police are here. Can you continue to try to persuade the rest of them that it would be in their interest for me to try to find out who murdered Mrs. Tamworthy?"

"I'll do my best."

"In that case, I'll concentrate on the village today. Paul Chambers is the ringleader of the protesters. Where does he live?"

"He owns the pub. He lives upstairs."

"Does the pub belong to the estate?"

"Yes, and the rest of the village."

"Now the two women who served lunch. What are their names and where do they live?"

"One is Doris Crampton. She lives in Pear Tree Cottage. The other is her sister, Mavis. They live together. They do the cleaning here and my mother-in-law would engage them when we all met here for meals to wait at table. Oh, it's all so awful. There are police out scouring the countryside for hemlock."

"Will they find it?"

"I should think so. It's pretty common."

"How do you know that?" asked Agatha sharply.

"We Googled it on Fran's computer this morning."

"I'll collect Toni and be off to the village."

As Agatha drove out and checked signposts to Lower Tapor—the easy entrance to the manor was in Upper Tapor—she asked Toni, "Well, what did you make of them?"

"I can't quite believe it," said Toni. "It's like a stage set. They don't belong. I dunno. I mean, they look like a group of people who've gone to one of those hotels where they do murder weekends. You know, where they dress up in thirties costumes and one of them plays Poirot. They look as if they're waiting to put their costumes on and wondering which one of them is going to play the murderee.

"I don't know anything about manor houses, but I thought they would look more at ease in their surroundings. Of course the place itself is more like a hotel."

"Evidently Fran and Sadie have grand ideas and both would like to be ladies of the manor," said Agatha. "But surely not that manor house. But I doubt if either of them would want to buy the others out. Unless, of course, Sir Henry Field is rich. Alison said she has her own money. I wonder just how much she has got. Here we are at the pub. Be prepared to be insulted."

A few locals stared at them sullenly as they walked into the stone-flagged bar. Paul Chambers was behind the bar sitting on a high stool, reading a newspaper.

He looked up at Agatha and his eyes hardened. "I heard about you," he said. "Some sort of snoop."

"I am a private detective employed by the family to find out who murdered Mrs. Tamworthy," said Agatha.

He had unusually pale eyes and a shock of fair hair and fair lashes. "You're looking in the wrong place," he said. He looked at Toni. "You employing child labour these days?"

"Watch your mouth, mate," snarled Toni, and Agatha looked at her in surprise.

But Paul grinned. "Feisty, aren't you? It's no use bothering me."

"You were furious at Mrs. Tamworthy when you learned she planned to sell the place," said Agatha.

"Yeah. But I wouldn't have murdered the old trout. What good would it do? None of that lot has enough money to keep the place going."

"What about Bert Tamworthy? He runs the brickworks."

"Sure, but the brickworks are part of the estate, see?"

"What about Sir Henry Field?"

"Got a little money from a family trust. Enough to keep him from working for a living, but that's all."

"How do you know this?"

"Made it my business."

"Are you sure Mrs. Tamworthy had planning permission to build houses on her land?"

"Sure. There's a field that's never used other side of the six-acre. There's ruined houses there. There were about ten of them in the nineteenth century. The manor was owned then by a Jeremy Twistle. He chucked the tenants out because he wanted the extra land for agriculture. But he died before he could do anything about it and the houses fell into ruin. Mrs. Tamworthy claimed that as the land had never been used for agriculture, she had a right to build on it and got planning permission. We weren't having any of that."

"Why?" asked Agatha. "The countryside is short of housing."

"It's damn short of affordable housing," said Paul. "She'd build houses for rich incomers and we've got enough incomers in the Cotswolds driving house prices up so that the villagers can't afford to live in them."

"If the villagers would stop selling their homes to incomers," said Agatha, "then the prices wouldn't become inflated."

"What do you know about anything? Shove off."

"Were you up at the manor house yesterday?" asked Toni.

"No, I wasn't, cheeky-face."

"And you can prove it?"

"Course I can, but I'm not going to waste time telling a slip of a girl like you. Tell you what, come back this evening when you've got rid of granny here, and maybe I'll stand you a drink."

"I'll think about it," said Toni.

Agatha felt very low as they left the pub. She was in her early fifties, her legs were good and her hair glossy, but set against the glowing youth of Toni, she didn't stand a chance.

She swallowed her pride and said, "Maybe you should take him up on his offer."

"Where will you be?" asked Toni. "I doubt if there are any buses around here."

"We'll interview the sisters and then I think we should go back and pack overnight bags. I'll find a hotel near here and book us in. I'll drop you off at the pub and I'll be able to start work at the manor early the next morning."

She drove slowly around the small village until they located Pear Tree Cottage.

One of the sisters answered the door. "Oh, it's you," she said. "What d'yer want?"

She was, as Agatha remembered her, fat and frumpy. Her hair was tied up in a scarf and she had an old-fashioned flowery apron stretched across her bulk.

"I am a private detective," said Agatha. "I wanted to ask you a few questions about yesterday."

The woman raised her voice and screeched, "Doris!" Her sister came into the room. "Here's a nosy parker come to ask us about yesterday," said Mavis.

"Cheek!" said Doris. "Get along with you. You ain't the perleece." She seized a broom from the corner and brandished it. "Git!"

So Agatha and Toni retreated. Agatha decided to ask Phil Marshall to call on them. He might fare better.

The hotel that Agatha found for them early that evening struck Toni as being more like a manor house than the Tamworthy one. It was very expensive and she tried not to feel intimidated.

When they had checked in, Agatha said, "I'll drive you to the pub and call back for you in an hour. Then we'll have dinner. I've had nothing but a sandwich all day."

Toni felt that her luck had run out. The pub was busy and this time there was a woman behind the bar with Paul. She was gypsy-looking with ratty dead-black hair, a thin mouth, glistening black eyes and a formidable bosom.

"Here you are," Paul greeted her. "What are you having?"

"Tonic water."

"Have some gin in it."

"Maybe later."

"Paul. We've got other customers waiting," shouted the barmaid.

Paul winked at Toni. "That's Elsie, jealous as sin."

"Your wife?"

"No, but she'd like to be."

"Paul!"

"Come back at midnight," whispered Paul. "Meet me outside. I can tell you a lot."

"Right you are," said Toni. She drank her tonic, retreated outside the pub and phoned Agatha.

When Agatha arrived, Toni told her about the proposed meeting.

"Does he know you don't have a car?"

"Don't think so," said Toni.

"We'll go back to the hotel for dinner and then I'll come back with you at midnight and drop you near the pub."

Toni was glad of Agatha's robust presence in the hotel dining room. The waiter was supercilious until Agatha told him to take that look off his frost-bitten face and give them some decent service. She said this in a very loud voice. He was replaced by a servile waitress.

"They do try to give themselves airs," said Agatha. "It's all the fault of the English. They don't think a place is classy unless they're being humiliated. Mind you, this pepper steak is excellent. I wonder if they do catering. I planned to cook my Christmas dinner myself, but perhaps it might be safer to let someone else do it."

"Do you have a traditional Christmas?" asked Toni wistfully.

"Not yet. But I'm going to have one this time. I want a real Dickensian one with turkey and holly and, oh, you know"—Agatha waved her arms—"the whole thing."

"We never had a proper Christmas," said Toni.

"Well, you can help me with mine. I'm hoping my ex will be back from his travels in time for it."

"Your ex?"

"James Lacey. He's a travel writer."

"So it was an amicable divorce?"

"Yes, we're friends now. But I really think he's never got over me."

"Have you got over him?" asked Toni.

"Eat your steak."

Later that evening, Agatha drove Toni near the village pub but where her car could not be seen. Before Toni got out of the car, Agatha handed her a can of pepper spray. "Just in case he tries anything funny. Keep it in your hand."

Toni got out and walked towards the pub. It was a bright moonlit night. Paul was standing beside a four-wheel drive.

"Get in," he said. "We'll go somewhere where we can talk."

Agatha, who had followed behind on foot, saw Toni getting into the car and ran back to her own.

Paul drove off slowly and quietly and then, once clear of the pub, he accelerated, racing down country lanes until he finally swung off on a farm track and parked in a field.

He switched off the engine and turned towards Toni, putting his arm along the back of the passenger seat.

"What I want to ask you . . ." began Toni bravely.

"Forget that. Come here. Let's have a bit of fun."

"No," said Toni.

To her horror, he put his hands round her neck and began to squeeze. "You just be a good little girl and be nice to Paul."

Toni felt she was losing consciousness. With a great effort, she raised the can of pepper spray, thrust it up between them and sprayed it full into his face.

He let out a roar like a wounded bull. Toni pulled open the door and collapsed out onto the grass. Howling and cursing, he stumbled out as well.

"I'll kill you, you little bitch," he raged.

And then there came the roar of a car engine. Agatha had desperately followed, glad of the moonlit night because she had been following without lights on, hoping that the sound of Paul's engine would drown the sound of her own. As soon as she heard his engine stop, she had stopped her own.

When she heard him shouting, she accelerated towards the sound of the voice. She saw Toni stumbling to her feet and Paul weaving about, his hands to his eyes.

"Stop!" yelled Agatha. "I have a gun."

Through his bleary painful eyes, Paul saw Agatha Raisin holding a gun pointed at him.

"Get up against the car!" roared Agatha.

"It was a joke, that's all," he said.

"Put your hands behind your back."

Muttering curses, Paul did as he was told. Agatha clipped a pair of handcuffs on him. Then she took a belt from her dress and bound his ankles.

"Are you all right, Toni?" she asked.

"He tried to strangle me," croaked Toni. "I can hardly breathe."

"Sit down on the grass. I'll call the police."

It was to be a long night. Toni made a brief statement and was taken off to hospital for observation. Agatha was taken to police headquarters and grilled. She had removed the handcuffs when she heard the police siren in the distance. She did not know whether it was legal for a member of the public to use them or not, even though the sex shops sold them. She had hurled the pepper spray into the bushes, and had placed a half-empty carton of black pepper on the passenger seat. Pepper spray is illegal in the UK. She kept the half-empty carton of pepper with her in case she ever had to lie about the use of a pepper spray. She had briefed Toni before the girl was taken off to hospital to say that she had used a carton of pepper.

The hard-faced detective, Collins, was conducting the interview. "How did you get a powerful man like Paul Chambers to stand there with only a dress sash about his ankles while you phoned us?"

"He thought I had a gun."

"And did you?"

Agatha opened her handbag and produced a water pistol. "Just this. He couldn't see very well with the pepper in his eyes."

"Why was your assistant conveniently carrying a carton of black pepper in her handbag?"

"We were eating pepper steak earlier at the hotel. Toni opened her handbag and showed me the carton. She said that, funnily enough, she meant to try to cook pepper steak for herself."

"I think you are lying," said Collins.

Agatha lost her temper. "Prove it! Look here, you can see from the marks on her neck that my assistant was attacked. I suggest you concentrate on the real villain and stop wasting my time."

After a half-hour of questioning, Collins ended the tape and said in a cold measured voice, "I do not like you, Mrs. Raisin, or your methods. I must ask you not to interfere in this case or I will charge you with obstructing the police in their duties."

"I have been engaged by a member of the family to solve Mrs. Tamworthy's murder," protested Agatha.

"Just get out. I don't want to see you again."

SIX

†

TONI WAS released from hospital the following morning. She went to her flat and changed her clothes and then went to the office. Agatha squawked with dismay when she saw her.

"Get out of here," said Agatha. "I'm feeling guilty enough about you as it is. Go on. Have a good rest."

But Toni, weighed down with gratitude for her flat and her job, refused to go. "I'm a bit hoarse," she said, "but it's only bruising."

"If you're sure . . ."

"Very sure."

Patrick and Phil were there, notebooks at the ready.

"Now, what have we got?" said Agatha. "I feel sure the motive must have been money. Bert's brickworks are not doing well. Might be an idea, Patrick, to snoop around and find out why. Houses are being put up all over the place. Has he been gambling? Keeping a bit of totty on the side? His wife says she has her own money. How much? I wonder. And what did that country lady see in the very lower-middle-class Bert?

"Sir Henry just has a relatively small amount from a family trust. Does he work? Maybe you can find out, Phil, but before that I want you to go to Lower Tapor and see if you can chat up the two village women who were serving the meal on the last day of Mrs. Tamworthy's life. I'll give you their names and their address. I think you might have better luck there than I did."

Agatha turned to Toni. "I would feel easier if you would take on some of the lesser jobs today. We still have two dogs missing and three cats. Mrs. Freedman will give you the details."

Toni opened her mouth to protest but then quickly decided that as the most junior employee, she should do as she was told.

Agatha set out again for the manor. She wondered what Charles was doing. Certainly he had dropped in and out of her past before, but he had always stuck with each case—well, more or less.

There was a slight chill in the air. Castles of white clouds rode high above in a pale-blue sky. Perhaps, thought Agatha, just for once it might be a cold winter. Perhaps there might even be snow. She could see it now, her house full of happy guests, holly and mistletoe, a roaring log fire and James, tall and handsome, smiling down at her.

She swung round a bend and nearly collided with a tractor. She mounted the verge to let the tractor pass, swearing under her breath. The tractor driver from his higher perch looked down at her insolently, a cigarette dangling from his lower lip.

Agatha was suffering from not enough sleep. "Moron!" she shouted.

The man's eyes narrowed and he began to climb down from the tractor. Agatha wrenched the wheel, managed to get past the tractor and accelerated off. She could see his face, contorted with fury, in her rear-view mirror.

I must watch my temper, thought Agatha. If Paul Chambers gets out on bail, then I'll have enough danger from the local yokels without courting more.

Only Alison, Fran and Sadie were at the manor. "Where is everybody?" asked Agatha.

"Bert has gone to the brickworks," said Alison. "Henry's gone up to London, and Jimmy's gone to close up the shop and put it up for sale."

"Will Bert continue to run the brickworks now he doesn't have to?" asked Agatha.

"No, he wants to sell. He never liked the job anyway."

Agatha glanced at Fran and Sadie. They seemed to be making up lists.

"Fran and Sadie are making lists of everything to divide up. Not that there's really anything of value. Come through to the morning room," said Alison.

The morning room conjured up in Agatha's mind a charming refuge full of sunlight and comfortable chairs. But when Alison pushed open a door and ushered her in, she found herself in a small, dusty, dark room. The darkness was caused by a pile of boxes against the window. The only furnishings were a small round table covered with a dingy lace cloth and two battered leather chairs.

"I see nobody used this room," said Agatha.

"Mother-in-law preferred the drawing room. The manor

was too large for her. She would have been happier in a small bungalow, but she was devoted to the memory of my father. He bought this place and so she was determined to stay."

"And yet she had recently changed her mind?"

Alison sighed. "I sometimes wonder if she really liked her own children. None of them were happy. Jimmy hated the shop. Bert did his best with the brickworks, but after a time he began to lose interest."

"I heard the business wasn't doing too well."

"He wasn't gambling or anything. He was beginning to be late with orders and builders were moving their business to other brickworks. He'll be glad to get out of it."

"If you will forgive me for saying so," said Agatha, "you seem an ill-assorted pair."

For a moment, Alison looked angry. Then she shrugged. "I was brought up on a farm. Although my father was rich and a gentleman farmer, he liked us—that's me and my sister, Hetty, and brother, George—to do the farm work. I hated it. I'm no oil painting and the other rich farmers' sons wanted to marry pretty girls. I met Bert at the Moreton-in-Marsh agricultural show. I was sitting by myself in the beer tent. The other tables were crowded and he asked if he could join me. We got talking and we soon had a mutual bond discussing bullying parents. He hated the brickworks and I hated farming. One thing led to another and we got engaged. He was my ticket out of farming. He said if I married him I wouldn't need to see another cow or sheep again.

"Phyllis—Mrs. Tamworthy—was against me from the start. At my wedding she was on her worst behaviour and my family were furious. She actually got drunk, insisted on making a speech, and ran Bert down in front of everyone."

"He must have hated her," said Agatha.

"But he didn't kill her," said Alison fiercely. "He always made allowances for her."

"What about Jimmy? Now, he hated that shop."

"That was a bit of cruelty I'll never understand," said Alison. "She appeared to dote on him."

"And he never married?"

"Bert said when Jimmy was younger, there were a couple of girls interested in him, but Phyllis soon saw them off. He found out later when one of the girls was married to someone else that Phyllis had told her that Jimmy was subject to bad epileptic fits."

"What about Fran? She's divorced. Did Phyllis have anything to do with that?"

"Not really. Fran longed to belong to the upper classes. She met this stockbroker, Peter Meadows. He was such a snob. She met him on holiday and they got married abroad. By the time he got to know her family, he turned nasty and said they were common. But she was pregnant, so the marriage struggled on for a few years until the divorce. He was a pill, but Fran blamed her mother for not being posh enough."

"Dear me. And Sadie?"

"Sadie seems happy with Henry, but he doesn't have much money and Phyllis would not give her anything for her daughter's education. Lucy had to go to a comprehensive. Oh dear, I seem to be giving you a lot of motives for murder. But I know these people. I keep thinking it was someone from the village who took away the parsnips and substituted them with hemlock. I thought before that the tale of the death of Socrates we got at school was all bumpkin or the Greeks must have mixed the hemlock with something else. But there was a case in Perthshire in the nineteenth century where a farmer's children had made up his sandwiches with what they thought was parsley but was hemlock. The top of the plant is just as poisonous as the root. He died just the same way as Phyllis. No convulsions, no vomiting, just slow paralysis."

"How do you know this?"

"We've all been looking up hemlock poisoning on our computers."

"Is there any hope," asked Agatha, "that Phyllis might have made the mistake herself?"

"Won't do. If that were the case, we'd all have been poisoned."

"Are the rest of them quite happy with the idea of my investigating the murder?"

"Yes, they've all come round, except Henry, who thinks it's all a waste of money."

"You say you have your own money. Couldn't you have made Bert give up the brickworks?"

"He was just about to. He wouldn't do it before because he feared his mother's contempt."

"Does your father still have the farm?"

"No, he died. Terrible accident. He climbed up the grain silo for some reason and fell in. He was smothered in the grain. He left us all a great deal of money. He had invested well and he was a bit of a miser."

Agatha's brain was beginning to whirl with all this information. She had a nasty little picture of Alison climbing up the silo after her father and shoving him in.

"Isn't it odd?" said Alison. "These days the world is full of therapy-speak and you hear people on television saying that they come from a dysfunctional family. What is a functional one, I wonder. Does it exist?"

"I'm in the wrong line of business to tell you that," said Agatha.

Toni, mindful of Mrs. Freedman's earlier instructions, went to the animal refuge and located all the missing animals except one cat.

As she did not have transport, she thought of phoning up the owners and telling them to call at the refuge. She phoned Mrs. Freedman. "Don't do that, dear," said Mrs. Freedman. "You'll make it look too easy. You wait there and I'll be round with my car."

To Toni's relief, Mrs. Freedman turned up in a Land Rover. They borrowed carrying cases from the refuge, bore the animals off to the office and phoned the delighted owners.

When the last one had gone, Mrs. Freedman said to Toni, "You're looking a bit peaky. Why don't you run along to your flat and have a nice lie-down."

Toni retreated to her flat. She made herself a light lunch and then slept for two hours and awoke feeling much refreshed but also restless. Her friends must be wondering where she had got to. Since joining the agency, she had not seen any of them, partly because she had been busy and partly out of fear that her brother might track her down if he learned where she was. Would her name be in the newspapers? It would have been too late for the attack on her to be reported in that day's newspapers. But what about tomorrow? Then she relaxed. They would probably just say that a man had been charged with attempted rape. Her name would not be mentioned until the court case came up.

*   *   *

Doris Crampton opened her cottage door to see who had knocked. An inoffensive elderly man stood on the doorstep.

"I am Phil Marshall," said Phil politely. "I am helping to investigate the murder of Mrs. Tamworthy."

"Are you police?"

"No. Private detective."

Doris made as if to close the door. But Phil looked so unthreatening with his white hair ruffled by the breeze and Doris had a longing to gossip.

"Come in," she said, "but I can't really tell you anything."

Phil followed her into the cottage parlour. "You have a nice home here," he said.

"For how long?" demanded Doris.

"Why do you ask?"

"Because we pay rent to the manor, see. When the whole place is sold, the new owner might turf us out. I'll say one thing for Mrs. Tamworthy, she never raised the rents. That's why we was all so upset when we heard she was planning to sell. It waren't really nothing to do with the building plot."

"Dear me. It must all be very worrying for you," said Phil.

"Sit down," said Doris. Phil sat down in an armchair beside the fireplace and Doris took the seat opposite him.

"I find it surprising that Mrs. Tamworthy didn't raise the rents," commented Phil. "From what I've heard about her, she seems to have been a hard-nosed businesswoman."

"She was that. But you know, sir, I don't think she did it out o' kindness. Kept reminding all of us how generous she was and there was always at the back of her voice and in her eyes a sort of threat. We was all frightened to cross her. I think she liked her bit o' power. But no one in the village would have harmed her. I mean getting rid of her would mean her children taking over and there would be nothing to stop them raising the rents or selling the place."

"But she was going to sell anyway," Phil pointed out.

"We kept hoping she'd come round. See, she liked upsetting people."

"To get to the murder," said Phil. "Did she always make that salad herself?"

"Right proud of it, she were. There's a big kitchen garden up at the manor and she'd go herself to get the vegetables. There's a gurt big shed at the end where the picked fruit and vegetables are stored."

"There is a gardener, of course?"

"Yes, that's Fred Instick. He's getting on and the work's hard. He kept asking for an undergardener but she wouldn't listen to him. Told him to get Jill, the groom, to help. Jill did it sometimes because she was sorry for Fred but usually pointed out she had her hands full with the horses. He'll be worried about his house, now. Don't think anyone now'll want to keep on an old gardener."

"I'd like to meet him. Where is his cottage?"

"It's at the back of the stables."

Said Phil, "You say Mrs. Tamworthy was very proud of her salad and yet she did not serve it at dinner."

"No, sir, always at high tea. She said it were right good for her bowels."

"How did she get on with her children?"

"They didn't come round much. Just on her birthday and Christmas. 'Cept for Jimmy. He was round a lot."

"It's a big house. Didn't he live with her?"

"No, poor sod lived above the shop. She charged him rent, too."

Phil looked shocked. "I'm really not surprised someone has murdered her."

Doris smiled for the first time. "Let me get you some tea, sir."

Fran had agreed to be interviewed by Agatha. She sat in front of Agatha, nervously plucking at her skirt.

"At first," said Fran, "we were really all against you trying to find out who murdered Mother. But then the police began to make each one of us feel guilty. Something's got to be done. Jimmy's going ahead putting the shop up for sale. It's too early. None of us is going to get a good price with the suspicion of murder hanging over our heads. Besides, it's just a little shop, no post office counter. The villagers go on grumbling about keeping the old ways but most of them shop at the supermarkets. The ones who go to Jimmy get their groceries on tick and then he has the awful job of making sure they pay their bills."

"Was your mother—how can I put this—was she ever very maternal?"

"Not that I can remember. Dad adored us. We had marvellous Christmases when we were small. It was only after he died that Mother—well—*turned*. I sometimes wonder if she was jealous of us all."

"Was Jimmy always destined to be a shopkeeper?"

"No, he was working in computers as a website developer, a firm in Mircester. The firm went bust just after Dad died. He was looking around for another job when Mother bulldozed him into running the shop."

"The shop did not belong to the estate?"

"No, she bought it for him and gave it to him as a Christmas present. You should have seen his face. I thought he was about to cry."

"And Bert?"

"Well, Dad had taken him into the business and he was happy working with him."

"And you are divorced?"

"Yes. He *was* snobbish but it was as if Mother went out of her way to look common when he was around. She wouldn't help out with Annabelle's education."

"Didn't you get a good settlement from the divorce?"

Fran turned red. "I had an affair. I looked on it as a passing fling, but my ex got a private detective on to it. He said if I didn't just walk away from the marriage, he would bring out my adultery in court. I should have stood my ground and fought for some money for Annabelle's education, but I was so ashamed and Mother said, 'Don't worry about it. I'll give you an income.' It wasn't enough."

"When your daughter grew up, did she come to resent her grandmother?"

"Annabelle doesn't resent anyone. A girlfriend with money suggested they open a dress shop in the King's Road in Chelsea. It did and does very well."

"Annabelle isn't married?"

"My daughter is a lesbian."

"Oh. Do you own your own house?"

"No. Mother bought it for me. Or rather, she bought it and

took the rent out of my allowance. It's a poky former council house in Mircester."

"And you all knew about your mother's special salads?"

Fran shrugged. "Couldn't not. As far as I can remember, she's served up the beastly things."

"But you'll be able to sell the house now?"

"Yes, thank God. We're going to all try to stay here at the manor until this dreadful murder is solved. It must be someone from the village."

"Why?"

"Because none of us has the guts. She really ground us down."

"Is the kitchen door always open during the day?"

"Yes, anyone could have come in that way. You know what these villages are like. Lots of inbreeding. I think it was done by someone mad."

"Where is Jimmy at the moment?"

"He's up at the shop, clearing out."

"Perhaps I might go up there for a word with him. And then perhaps Sadie might like to talk to me."

"I really don't think my sister or Bert can tell you anything further."

Agatha had to park a little way away from the shop. There was a crowd outside and the road was almost blocked by tractors and cars.

She walked forward and pushed her way to the front of the crowd. A rejuvenated Jimmy was shouting, "Everything must go. Fifty pee a box."

He's practically giving the stuff away, thought Agatha.

Groceries and vegetables from the shop had been piled into separate boxes. The boxes were disappearing rapidly as the villagers bought and bought, carrying stuff back to their cars and tractors and returning for more.

Jimmy's thin face was flushed and his eyes were shining. Hardly the grieving son, thought Agatha. She retreated to her car and decided to wait. It wouldn't be long before everything was gone.

One by one, the vehicles laden with groceries began to move off. Agatha's stomach rumbled. She fished in the glove compartment of her car and found a Mars bar, ate it and lit a cigarette.

When the last vehicle had gone, she climbed stiffly from her car, her treacherous hip sending pain shooting down her leg. She limped towards the shop and then heaved a sigh of relief as the pain subsided.

"Mr. Tamworthy?"

Jimmy, who was closing the shop door, turned round. "Oh, it's you."

"I wanted to ask you a few questions, if that's all right."

He hesitated and then said reluctantly, "You'd better come in, but I don't think I can be of much help."

He led the way into the shop. The wooden shelves were empty of groceries. A few newspapers and a cabbage stalk lay on the floor. Agatha followed Jimmy through the shop, into the back shop, and up a wooden staircase. He opened a door at the top and ushered her in.

She found herself in a bleak little room. Jimmy sat down at a round table at the window. Agatha sat down opposite him. She looked around. There were no books or paintings. The table she was sitting at was flanked by three hard upright chairs. A battered sofa and coffee table were placed in front of a television set. She wondered whether his bedroom might contain more signs of individuality.

Jimmy's face was a polite blank.

"Can you think of anyone at all who might have wanted to kill your mother?" began Agatha.

"Mum irritated a lot of people but not enough to make anyone want to kill her."

"Did she have trouble with anyone apart from the villagers recently?"

He shook his head. Then he said, "Blertyn's were annoying her a bit."

"Who are they?"

"A building developer. He was anxious to start building on the bit of land where those ruined houses are. Mum kept telling him to wait. The boss, Joe Trump, he said that recession was coming and if she didn't hurry up, he'd be unable to sell the houses. He was quite threatening."

"Where can I find Blertyn's?"

"Out on the industrial estate at Mircester."

"You must have hated your mother for having stuck you in this shop," said Agatha.

"She was my mother. You can't hate your own mother."

"It happens," said Agatha. "What will you do now?"

His brown eyes gleamed. "I'll travel. I'll go to all the places I ever wanted to see."

"When is the funeral?"

"We don't know. The police said they would let us know when they are releasing the . . . the . . . body."

His eyes filled with tears and he shouted, "I was enjoying

myself. This was *my* day! Why did you have to come along and spoil everything?"

Suddenly nonplussed, Agatha rose to her feet and muttered, "I'll talk to you later."

She clattered down the wooden stairs and out through the shop. It had begun to rain. Long fingers of rain were trailing across the stubble of the fields.

Agatha cursed herself as she walked to the car. Why had she run away like that? A real detective would have persevered.

Toni looked down from the window of her flat that evening and shrank back as she saw her brother coming along the street with two of his mates. They were glancing up at the buildings, searching for something. She had a sickening feeling they were looking for her.

She took another cautious look. She had phoned a friend, Maggie Spears, earlier and had asked her to come round. To her horror, she saw the three stop and start to talk to Maggie. Maggie said something, tossed her head and walked on. Then, to Toni's relief, Maggie walked straight past the entrance to the flats.

Five minutes later, Toni's phone rang. It was Maggie. "That no-good brother of yours was asking where you were. I'll come back when it's safe. I told him you lived in Beacon Street, you know, out on the Evesham Road."

"Thanks, Maggie," said Toni. "I'll be glad to see you."

SEVEN

†

PHIL DROVE up to the manor, parked discreetly behind the stables as he saw a police car approaching and went in search of the gardener, Fred Instick.

He found Fred, a gnarled old man, sitting on the edge of a wall smoking his pipe, seemingly unmindful of the steady drizzle falling down from the leaden sky above.

"I am a private detective," said Phil. "Is there anywhere we can talk out of the rain?"

Fred, by way of reply, walked off in the direction of a potting shed at a corner of the garden.

Phil took down the large golf umbrella he had been holding over his head and followed Fred inside.

Fred looked gloomily at his wet pipe, gave it a shake, put it down and drew out a packet of cigarettes.

Phil waited until he had lit a cigarette and then asked, "Do you know of anyone who would be likely to have murdered Mrs. Tamworthy?"

Fred puffed slowly at his cigarette. His face was as dry and brown and cracked as a bed of earth in a drought. "Reckon I might ha' done it," he said at last.

"Why?"

"Starvation pension, that's why. Her said she'd pay me cash. 'Don't want to worry about taxes, Fred,' that's what her did say. Now she's gone and them'll sell up and what'll I do? They'll sell my cottage and I ain't got a pension worth looking at cos there's no official record of me being employed."

Phil, who was in his seventies, looked sympathetically at the old gardener. Then he had an idea. Agatha paid him a generous salary and expenses.

"Look here, it's hard to try to get information about what goes on in the manor. We'd gladly pay you for anything you can find out."

"You mean like snooping?"

"Hard word, but that's what detective work is all about."

"I could do with the money. I've had a right hard time of it with the police grilling me and demanding to know if I supplied hemlock by accident along with the other vegetables."

"Here's my card," said Phil. "Any little thing you can think of. Keep your ears open. You're sure you don't have any idea who did the murder?"

"I think it were her youngest, Jimmy. The others lived away from the manor, but he were right up the road. Some mother that old woman was."

"Right, let me know if you think of anything else."

As Phil left the potting shed, the rain had increased to a

steady downpour. He got into his car and drove round to the front of the manor. The police car was still there, but no sign of Agatha's car. He decided to go back to the office and write up his notes.

Fred made his way up to the manor house with a basket of vegetables. He went in by the kitchen door and laid the basket on the table. He could hear them all talking in the drawing room. He felt sour and bitter. There they all were, having inherited a fortune while he was facing the remainder of his days in poverty.

Some mad impulse made him poke his head round the drawing room door. "Veggies in the kitchen," he said.

Fran said grandly, "Thank you, Fred, you may go."

Her lady-of-the-manor attitude made Fred furious. "I know which one of you did it," he said. White, shocked faces turned in his direction. He grinned and slammed the door. On his way out through the kitchen, he saw bottles of Mrs. Tamworthy's wine in a rack by the door. He helped himself to a bottle and retreated to his cottage.

Agatha was cross with Charles for disappearing. She was at last fed up with the fact that he had the keys to her cottage and could come and go as he liked.

The following morning she telephoned the security firm that had installed her burglar alarm and asked them to come immediately to change the locks on her door and the code on the burglar alarm.

She telephoned the office and said she would be a bit late.

When the workmen arrived, she said she was going out for half an hour and made her way up to the vicarage.

"I'm getting the locks on my cottage changed," said Agatha as soon as Mrs. Bloxby opened the door.

"So no more surprise visits from Sir Charles?"

Agatha followed her into the vicarage living room. "I don't like the way he uses my house as a hotel."

"Mrs. Raisin, I do believe you are—" Mrs. Bloxby broke off. She had been about to say "growing up at last." She changed it to "being very sensible. Have you time for a coffee?"

"Yes, please, but only if it's ready. I can't be away too long."

"It's ready. Won't be a minute."

"May I smoke?"

"Not in the house. We can go into the garden. It's a fine morning."

"Don't bother. The table and chairs will still be wet after last night's rain."

"It's all right. I've wiped them down."

Agatha went out into the garden. The air was fresh and scented with autumn flowers. She took a deep breath, thinking how good country air was for her health, and then lit a cigarette.

"I heard on the local radio station," said Mrs. Bloxby when she returned with two cups of coffee, "that Paul Chambers is out on bail."

"Damn! I'll need to keep Toni well away from that village. It's a pity because the girl has a sharp eye."

"Tell me how far you've got with the case."

Agatha began to sum up the little she knew. "Dear me,"

said Mrs. Bloxby when she had finished, "one would think Mrs. Tamworthy *wanted* to be murdered."

"The thing that puzzles me," said Agatha, "is why was she clutching that hemlock root? I mean, how did she get hold of it? Surely the killer wouldn't go out of his way to give us a clue as to how she had been poisoned?"

"It's all very odd," said Mrs. Bloxby.

Agatha looked at her watch and let out a squawk. "I'd better go. They should be finished by now."

When Agatha finally got to the office, she carefully read the notes from Phil and Patrick. Patrick had written that Alison appeared to have been correct when she said her husband had lost interest in the brickworks. The failure of the brickworks did seem to have been caused by Bert not paying much attention to orders.

Sir Henry Field came as a surprise. He was managing director of a firm that made health-food bars, a small concern. Patrick had gathered that he didn't have much to do with the running of the firm. The owner liked Henry's title on their masthead.

Agatha, when she had read Phil's notes, said, "I find this gardener interesting. I would like to talk to him myself. It'll keep us clear of the house if the police are still around. Patrick, if you could get back to some of the other cases . . . We're getting a backlog. Toni, you go through the cases with him and see what you can do."

Patrick said, "Agatha, Toni is seventeen. You can drive a car at seventeen."

"I thought it was eighteen!"

"So did I," said Toni. "I mean, if you have no hopes of owning a car, you don't think much about ages."

"Right. Toni, get Mrs. Freedman to book you up for a crash driving course where you get your licence at the end of the week."

"I can't afford a car!" exclaimed Toni.

"I'll get you an old banger. It'll be the property of the agency. Get on with it. Come along, Phil. Let's cross your gardener's palm with silver and see what he comes up with."

"Police are still here," grumbled Agatha to Phil, who was driving.

"I'll park round the back," said Phil.

"Do you know where his cottage is?" asked Agatha.

Phil shook his head. "Don't worry. He's probably in the garden."

He parked the car and led the way to the kitchen garden. But there was no sign of Fred.

"I don't want to go into the house with the police there," said Agatha. "Let's go to the stables. That groom, Jill, will know where to find him."

They met Jill as she was crossing the stable yard. To Agatha's question, she said, "If you go right round the back of the kitchen garden to where those ruined houses are, you'll find his cottage just the other side of the ruins."

"Do you have any idea who might have wanted to kill Mrs. Tamworthy?" asked Agatha.

Jill put down the bucket and ran a hand through her short curly hair. "I've only worked here for three months. The previous groom left in a huff. Said she wasn't being paid enough and there was too much work for one person."

"And is there?"

"Not now," said Jill with a sigh. "Several owners have been up with their horse boxes to take their precious animals away. I'm starting to look for another job."

"They surely don't think anyone would murder the horses," said Phil.

Jill laughed. "If you owned several thousand pounds of horseflesh, you wouldn't be taking any chances either. They say that even if it turns out that the hemlock in the salad was an accident, then it follows that some of the stuff might get into the feed."

They thanked her and walked back to the kitchen garden, then round it and found themselves facing the field with the ruined houses. "That must be the cottage," said Phil, pointing to a small building on the other side of the field. "We'll need to cross the field."

Agatha was wearing flat sandals. The field was still sodden from the previous day's rain. She squelched across it following elderly Phil's athletic stride. Phil was wearing serviceable boots. How does he manage to keep so fit at his age? wondered Agatha. Maybe it's because he doesn't smoke. Must stop. Well, maybe tomorrow.

"Here we are," said Phil. "Real agricultural labourer's cottage. Cheap brick. Look, there's even a pump in the garden. Maybe he doesn't have any running water. I don't suppose he uses the front door. Let's try the side."

Phil knocked loudly on the door. They waited. Somewhere in the distance they could hear the sound of a tractor. Good heavens, thought Agatha. She said she had someone to manage the farming bit. Must find out who that is and where he lives.

Phil bent down and peered through the letter box. "I can hear the sound of a television set," he said. "Maybe the old boy fell asleep in front of it last night. The curtains on the windows are still drawn."

"Try the door," said Agatha.

Phil turned the handle and the door opened. "I don't suppose he bothers to lock up out here," he whispered. "What should we do?"

"Let me," said Agatha, pushing past him. She opened a door to the left off a tiny dark hall. Fred Instick was slumped in front of a small television set.

"Time to get up!" called Agatha.

The figure in the chair did not move.

Agatha swung round wildly. "Phil . . . ?"

"Let me," said Phil. He went forward and bent over the old gardener. His heart sank. Fred's eyes were wide open, staring sightlessly at Jerry Springer on the television set. He felt for a pulse on the man's neck. Then he straightened up. "He's dead, Agatha."

"Heart attack?"

"Look, there's a bottle of wine nearly empty on the little table beside his chair."

"We'd better not touch anything," said Agatha. "Let's get out of here and call the police."

Outside the cottage, Agatha took out her mobile phone and called the manor. Alison answered. "You'd better tell the police that the gardener, Fred Instick, is dead," said Agatha. Phil could hear the tones of Alison's shocked voice squawking down the line. Then Agatha said, "I know he was old, but the circumstances are suspicious. I think he was poisoned."

Agatha rang off and said, "Now we're in for a day of questioning. And I meant to go over to Blertyn's today."

"Who are they?"

"They're the builders. The ones who were going to build on that ruined-houses bit. Oh, here comes that bitch with Wilkes."

Detective Sergeant Collins came marching across the field towards them, followed by Inspector Wilkes.

When they arrived, Agatha said curtly, "Living room on the left as you go in."

"Wait here," snapped Collins. "We'll need you for questioning."

It was a long dreary day. First Agatha and Phil waited at the manor while a forensic team and pathologist arrived. Then back came the mobile police unit and parked outside the manor.

Finally Bill put his head round the drawing room door and said, "Mrs. Raisin?"

As soon as they were in the hall, Agatha complained, "You said you were coming to see me to take my statement last time."

"Wilkes countermanded that," said Bill. "He wanted to interview you himself."

"Was Instick poisoned?"

"It looks like it. The top brass are coming to deliver a rocket to the forensic team. They were supposed to have examined everything in that kitchen."

The door opened and Collins stood there. "We are waiting to interview Mrs. Raisin," she said harshly, and then turned on her heel.

"Why not you?" asked Agatha.

"Collins is Wilkes's pet."

"Good God!"

"You'd better go. I will try to call round."

Agatha marched out towards the mobile police unit. It was going to be a long day.

She stopped just outside the unit and phoned Patrick. "Could you drop what you're doing and go and interview Blertyn's, the builders? They're in Mircester. Take Toni with you."

Patrick and Toni drove to Blertyn's offices out on the industrial estate. Toni was hugging herself with excitement. Mrs. Freedman had booked her a crash driving course for the following week.

"Here we are," said Patrick. "Let's see what they have to say for themselves."

The receptionist looked up in surprise as they walked in. "Toni!" she cried. "Wot you doin' here?"

"I'm a private detective," said Toni. "We're here to interview your boss."

"Go on!"

"Fact."

"Well, I never did. I s'pose you want to speak to Mr. Trump himself? He's the manager."

"That would be great, Sharon."

"What's he done? Cheating on his wife?"

"No, nothing like that. Just a routine inquiry. Tell you what, you get him for us and give me your phone number and we'll get together one evening."

"Great. Hang on. I'll get him." She picked up the phone.

"Just say," said Toni quickly, "that a Mr. Mulligan wishes to talk to him about a building plot."

"Got it, Sherlock. Take a seat."

Sharon made the call. That could have been me, thought Toni, working in a dead-end job like Sharon's. I'd be having fun if only I didn't feel so dreadfully grateful to Agatha.

"Better make like I don't know you," said Sharon, replacing the receiver. "His secretary's coming to get you and she's a tartar."

The door to the inner office opened and a tall thin bespectacled woman said, "Mr. Mulligan? If you will follow me."

Mr. Trump, who rose to meet them as they entered his office, obviously had nothing to do with the manual side of the job. He was plump and well tailored with a round bland face and thick grey hair.

"Please sit down," he said, indicating two chairs facing his desk, "and let me know how I can be of assistance."

He began to look like a petulant baby as Patrick explained the reason for their visit.

"I'm a busy man," he said crossly. "Mrs. Tamworthy was interested in selling me a plot of land for building development, but she would never close the deal although I offered her a good price. One day she would say that she was coming into the office to close the deal and then she would phone later to say she had changed her mind. I thought she'd gone senile. You'd be better off having a talk with her factor, George Pyson."

"Where do we find him?"

"He's got a small office in College Street. Number ten. I called on him one time to see if he could talk some sense into the old girl's head."

Patrick and Toni parked in the centre of Mircester and walked along College Street. Number ten was a small old former shop with bottle-glass windows. Patrick rang the bell and they waited.

The door was eventually answered by a tall man with a thick shock of black hair. He was wearing a checked shirt and green corduroy trousers. His face was handsome in a craggy way. He was younger than Patrick had expected. Patrick placed him as being somewhere in his thirties.

"Are you George Pyson?" asked Patrick.

"That's me."

"We're private detectives investigating the murder of Mrs. Tamworthy at the request of her family."

"You'd better come in. Who's this?"

"Miss Toni Gilmour, also a detective. I am Patrick Mulligan."

The small office had a desk and hard chairs. A map of the Tamworthy village and estate was pinned to the wall behind the desk.

"What precisely is your job?" asked Toni.

"I run the estate, collect the rents, do the farm books and hire the help."

"How long have you been doing the job?" asked Patrick. "I mean, you're much younger than I expected."

"Only for four years. The previous factor died."

"So for four years you have been working closely with the people of the village. Have you any idea who might have wanted to murder Mrs. Tamworthy?"

"I know an awful lot of people didn't like her. But murder? Hard to imagine anyone I've met actually doing it."

"Did you get on well with Mrs. Tamworthy?" asked Toni.

He surveyed her and smiled. "You're a pretty girl and would be prettier if you darkened your eyelashes."

"Leave my appearance out of this," protested Toni.

"Did I get on with her? She thought so, because I made the farming side pay. She flirted with me. Bit grotesque. Actually, I'm looking around for another job because I assume the heirs will be selling the place. It's an odd village."

"In what way?" asked Patrick.

"Closed, secretive. All the Cotswold villages have been in-filtrated by newcomers. Often there are more newcomers than villagers. But not in the Tapors. I think there might be a bit of inbreeding. Then there's witchcraft."

"Witchcraft!" exclaimed Toni and Patrick in unison.

"Just a feeling, maybe just an odd rumour here and there. There's a magazine that advertises when covens are meeting. It's supposed to be white magic. Harmless get-togethers. I looked it up once to see if Lower Tapor was mentioned, but nothing there. I'm sorry I can't be of any help to you. Leave me your cards and I'll phone you if I think of anything."

"What's the name of that magazine and where can I get one?" asked Toni.

"That shop in the High Street called The Other World, you know the one that sells magic rocks and incense sticks and things like that. You can pick one up there." He rose to show them out. "Young lady," he said to Toni, "I see that someone's given you a black eye recently. It's maybe a dangerous job for one so young."

"I manage," said Toni. He drew her back as Patrick, ahead of her, walked out into the street. "Do be careful."

"I can look after myself," said Toni tartly.

"What was that about?" asked Patrick as they walked towards the High Street.

"He told me to be careful. Cheek! He's old. Are we going to buy that magazine?"

"May as well," said Patrick. "He didn't say what it was called."

"I'm sure they'll know what it is."

The magazine turned out to be called *Your Magic*. They flipped to the back where there was a list of events. "Amazing," said Toni. "Covens all over the place. Must be a lot of sick people around. But nothing listed for Lower Tapor or anywhere near it."

Bill called on Agatha that evening. She welcomed him in, saying, "I began to wonder if I would ever see you again outside the line of duty."

"It's hard," he said. "You're hardly the flavour of the month."

"Want coffee?"

"I came to take you out to dinner—nowhere too expensive."

"Pub grub all right?"

"Fine."

"I feel like getting out of the village. The Bear in Moreton is okay, and if we sit in the bar I can smoke."

"Right, we'll take both our cars," said Bill. "I'll go straight home afterwards. My mother worries about me if she knows I'm not on duty and I'm out too late."

"Have you ever thought of getting a place of your own and being more independent?" asked Agatha.

Bill looked thoroughly surprised. "I don't see any reason to. I'm happy at home."

But you'll never get married if you continue to stay there. Your mother will see to that, thought Agatha.

Charles had heard about the latest murder on television. He packed a bag and drove to Agatha's cottage. He noticed her car was not outside so he decided to go in and wait for her. His keys would not work. He tried several times to open the door until it finally dawned on him that Agatha must have changed the locks.

Someone must have threatened her, thought Charles, not pausing for a moment to think that it might have anything to do with him.

He heaved his case back into the car. He decided to go back home through Moreton-in-Marsh in case Agatha had decided to do some late-night shopping at Tesco Express.

He saw her car parked outside the Black Bear, found a parking place for himself and strolled towards the pub.

"That's as much as I know, Bill," Agatha was saying. "The most interesting bit is Patrick's report of possible witchcraft."

"I don't see what's so interesting in that," said Bill.

"If people are as unhinged as to believe in witchcraft, then it follows that murder might be an easy step. What if several of the villagers were responsible? How did the hemlock get into the wine—it was hemlock, wasn't it?"

"Yes, they're pretty sure it was inserted through the cork with a syringe. Oh, here's Charles."

Charles breezed up. "Couldn't get into your cottage, Aggie. Tracked you down."

"I changed the locks just so that you couldn't drop in anytime you felt like it," said Agatha. "On several occasions you've frightened me when I came home and heard someone in the house."

Charles's normally light voice held an edge as he asked, "And didn't you think, as a friend, that it might be a nice idea to phone me and tell me?"

"Why do you always make me feel in the wrong?" said Agatha furiously.

"Because you are."

"I didn't even think to phone you," said Agatha, "because there is no point in doing so. Either Gustav, your man, or your aunt answers the phone and they both always say you are not at home even when you are."

"How right you are," said Charles, sitting down and opening a menu. "What's good here?"

"Try the sea bass or the lamb shank," said Bill, looking amused.

Agatha gave a little resigned shrug. "To get back to what we were talking about, the poison was put in the bottle with a syringe. I don't remember any corks on the bottles."

"They're plastic corks. Someone must have made an infusion of hemlock."

"Fingerprints?"

"Only the gardener's."

"And the rest of the bottles?"

"I don't know. They're examining them at the moment. Collins is screaming at forensics that they were supposed to have checked every item in that kitchen."

Charles ordered sea bass and a glass of white wine and leaned back in his chair. "It takes suspicion away from the family surely. I mean, they could have drunk it."

"I don't think so," said Agatha. "Mrs. Tamworthy insisted on serving it, but she was the only one who drank it. I took a sip and so did Charles, but we didn't like it so we didn't have any more. It's terribly sweet. The rest of the family didn't touch it at all."

"Well, they wouldn't, would they?" said Bill. "That is, if one of them or all of them knew about that poisoned bottle or bottles. But there's something very odd. Instick delivered vegetables to the manor and according to Alison, he put his head round the drawing room door where they were all gathered and said, 'I know which one of you did it.'"

"Oh dear, it really looks as if one of them is a murderer," said Agatha. "Bill, you said there were only Fred's fingerprints on the bottle. That means of course someone wiped the bottle clean before putting it back on the rack."

"Certainly looks that way."

Agatha had a sudden bright image of Jimmy, smiling and laughing as he practically gave away all the stock in the shop. She hoped it wouldn't turn out to be Jimmy who was the murderer. He'd already spent a good part of his life in one sort of prison.

"There's another thing. Paul Chambers is out on bail and

back in his pub with the locals ganging up behind him. You'd better keep young Toni away from that village."

Toni's mobile phone rang that evening. To her surprise it was George Pyson. "Feel like going out for a drink?" he asked.

Toni hesitated only a moment. She was tired of feeling too frightened to go out in Mircester in the evening in case she ran into her brother. George was a bit old but he had looked strong.

"All right," she said.

"I'd pick you up," said George, "but there was only your phone numbers on your card."

"I'll meet you somewhere."

"What about the George, like my name, in the centre?"

"Fine. Say, half an hour?"

"See you there."

Toni put on some light make-up. She had bought black mascara on the road home. She decided not to put it on. Might give the old boy some ideas.

When she entered the lounge bar of the George she wished she had dressed up instead of keeping on the jeans and white T-shirt she had been wearing all day. He had changed into a well-tailored suit, blue shirt and silk tie.

He really was quite handsome, she decided with surprise.

"What are you having?" he asked.

"Just a tonic water."

"Right." Toni was impressed by the fact that he hadn't urged her to take something stronger.

When he came back with the drinks, he began to talk about Lower Tapor, explaining, "I've been thinking and thinking if I might know anything that might help you. I went over there after you left and I talked to the tenant farmer, Kenneth Macdonald."

"Sounds Scottish."

"He is. The former tenant died leaving no heirs and so I advertised and got him. He's a good worker and honest. He's not accepted by the villagers and so he has a detached view of them. He says he's sure they practise witchcraft and are planning something for next Saturday night. He overheard two of the farmhands talking."

Toni's eyes gleamed with excitement. "Does he know where?"

"No, but there's a stand of trees on a hill above Lower Tapor. They're supposed to be fairy trees. I would guess there."

"I might go over and have a look at that," said Toni.

"Might not be safe. Remember, there's a murderer about." He fiddled with the stem of his wine glass. "I could go with you if you would like?"

"I've been told by my boss to keep away from the village," said Toni. "The landlord of the pub, Paul Chambers, tried to rape me."

"That's awful. I heard he was out on bail but the newspapers didn't give the name of the victim and the locals, apart from Kenneth, don't gossip to me. On the orders of the family, I've given him a month to pack up and get out. The family owns the pub. If they are going to wind up the estate, I could probably get a fair price for them from one of the breweries."

"He must really hate me now," said Toni. "I don't have a car, yet. I'm taking a crash course next week. Yes, I would like you to drive me there Saturday."

"Right, when you've finished your drink, I'll walk you home. I'll pick you up at around ten o'clock on Saturday evening. We'll need to find a good place to hide ourselves."

Toni was relieved when he walked her home chatting away about the estate, because he showed no signs of being interested in her sexually.

"I've just remembered something," said Agatha. "British sherry."

"What about it?" asked Bill.

"She said she loved draught British sherry. I don't think it's been around for years. So she must have stacked up on bottles and put them in the cellar."

Bill took out his mobile. "I'll be back in a moment. I'd better tell them to search the whole of the cellar."

When he had gone, Agatha turned to Charles. "Do you plan to stay with me?"

"That's the idea, Aggie."

"I'm not giving you a set of keys, mind?"

"Suit yourself, sweetie."

EIGHT

†

THE FOLLOWING day, Agatha phoned Alison and told her that there was no point in her going to the manor while the police were around and asked Alison if she could possibly get away and come to the office. Alison said she would be there in an hour's time.

Agatha decided her staff should work on other cases. Toni was sent in search of a missing teenager. She did not tell Agatha anything about the coming Saturday night. She was sure Agatha would refuse to let her go.

Patrick brightened when he was given a case of suspected industrial espionage at a sweet factory. The owners claimed that they were planning the launch of a new chocolate bar. The previous launch of a new health bar had been stolen by their competitors. "Anything to get away from divorce," said Patrick. Phil sighed. He was stuck with a divorce case.

Charles strolled into the office, helped himself to a coffee, and sat quietly in the corner.

When everyone had left except Agatha and Mrs. Freedman, Charles asked, "What now?"

"Alison should be here soon," said Agatha. "Better here than up at the manor with police and the enraged Collins prowling around. Now, be an angel and shut up while I get some paper-work done."

Charles folded his arms on his chest and promptly fell asleep.

"He must be tired," whispered Mrs. Freedman.

"He should be," retorted Agatha. "He was up all night watching old movies."

Charles woke up when Alison arrived. Agatha was shocked at her appearance. Her face was drawn and there were heavy bags under her eyes.

She sank down wearily on the office sofa. "I don't know how much longer we can all go on like this. The police are now searching the cellar."

"Were any of the other bottles on that rack in the kitchen poisoned?" asked Agatha.

"They don't know yet. George Pyson, the factor, is finding another gardener to fill in in the meantime. He has also found an accountant for us because it turns out Mrs. Tamworthy had lots of money salted away in different accounts. If we ever get out of this, we'll all be very rich indeed. But we'll never have any peace until this murderer is found. We're paying some of the villagers to patrol the estate because the press are doing everything they can to get in to interview us. When I drove off, I was nearly blinded by all the flashes from the cameras. Of course, the villagers have been talking, so George says, and it's probably all a lot of scurrilous gossip."

"What you need is a good foreign story," said Agatha cynically.

"I don't understand."

"If there's a big story abroad, you'll see the press trying to get back to their offices to buy the foreign editor drinks and free meals, begging, 'Send me. I've got a visa.' "

Charles had woken up. "Only Aggie could wish a war on the world for a bit of peace at Lower Tapor," he said.

Agatha ignored him. "Alison, I know you won't want to believe this, but if any of the Tamworthys had committed the murder, which one would you think it might be?"

"That's awful. Jimmy suffered the most but I can't see him doing it. I mean, it all looks as if it were carefully planned to hurt the family as much as possible. Poisoning that wine means the murderer was not just after my mother-in-law."

"Unless it was done before the murder," said Charles. "My money's on Paul Chambers. He seems a nasty bit of work. A man who would try to rape a young girl in the middle of a murder investigation must be a bit unhinged."

"Have you heard anything about witchcraft in the village?" asked Agatha.

"No," said Alison, "but then I never had much to do with the place."

"I know," said Agatha, "I'll phone Phil and send him back to see the Crampton sisters. He seems to have charmed them."

*   *   *

Phil was delighted to be able to temporarily drop the divorce case. As he drove into Lower Tapor and parked beside the village green, he could see no one about and yet was conscious of eyes staring at him from behind net curtains. He had never considered himself to be imaginative or psychic in any way and yet he could swear he felt the weight of the hidden watchers' curiosity and animosity.

Cotswold buildings weather very well. It was hard for Phil to guess the age of the houses. Some were thatched and timbered, so were probably seventeenth century or maybe earlier, their little dormer windows under the eaves looking like eyes. Others had slate roofs and lintels over the door in the style of Queen Anne.

He made his way past the pub to the sisters' cottage and knocked on the door. Once again Doris opened the door to him. She looked wary.

"I wonder if I might have another word with you," said Phil.

Doris leaned forward and looked to right and left and then said reluctantly, "Come in."

This time her sister, Mavis, was in the parlour. Phil was not asked to sit down. They both faced him, work-reddened hands folded over their aprons.

"I heard a rumour there was witchcraft in this village," said Phil.

They stared at him in silence and then Mavis turned and walked out.

"I don't know where you heard such rubbish," said Doris. "Now if you don't mind, I've got work to do."

"Terrible thing about Fred Instick," pursued Phil, not wanting to return to the office with nothing to report.

"That's what happens to nosy parkers," said Doris.

"You mean he had found something out and someone wanted to silence him?"

"Look," said Doris, "Fred was always bragging about what he called gardener's privileges. One of them was to help himself to a bottle of wine on his road out of the kitchen. He was the only one I knew who would touch the stuff. Mrs. Tamworthy did try to sell some at a village fête but nobody liked it. We make the good stuff here. It was sickly sweet and tasted a bit like medicine. I reckon her never allowed it to mature long enough. Now, get on with you."

Well, that was something to report, thought Phil. It looked as if the poisoning of the old man had been deliberate. He walked back to his car on the village green. Just as he opened the car door, something struck him viciously on the back of the head and he slumped to the ground, red blood trickling through the white hair on his head.

Two minutes later, George Pyson drove into the village. He saw Phil lying on the ground by his car, braked to a halt and got out and knelt beside him. He took out his phone and called urgently for an ambulance.

Bill Wong was the first on the spot. He had been driving to the manor and had heard the emergency call on the police radio.

George had taken a travel rug from the car and wrapped it around Phil. "There's a rock over there with blood on it," said George.

Bill phoned Agatha and told her what had happened. Then he asked, "What exactly was Phil doing in the village?"

Agatha told him that Phil had gone over to call on the

Crampton sisters. "It's Pear Tree Cottage," she said. "I'll be right over."

"Don't," said Bill. "Stay right where you are and I'll let you know which hospital they've taken him to."

George said, when Bill had rung off, "His pulse is steady enough. Where the hell's that ambulance?"

It was an agony of waiting until the ambulance arrived. "Taking him to Mircester General," said one paramedic.

As soon as the ambulance was out of sight, Bill turned to George. "Where is this Pear Tree Cottage?"

"I'll take you there."

But at Pear Tree Cottage no one answered the door. Bill flipped open the letter box and listened. He could hear a faint sound of movement from inside. He shouted through the letter box, "Police! Open up or I'll smash the door down."

Hurried footsteps could be heard on the other side. Then the door swung open and Doris stood there. "I was down in the garden," she said.

"The man who was just here," said Bill, "was struck in the head with a rock. Did you see anything?"

"That's awful. No, like I said, I was down in the garden."

"Did he ask you about witchcraft in the village?"

"Yes, that he did. Told him it was rubbish."

"Did he ask anything else?"

"No, I told him I was busy and he left."

Agatha paced up and down the waiting room of Mircester General Hospital. Phil was being examined. Bill and Charles were waiting with her.

"Collins is furious with you," Bill said. "She says you're complicating the case."

"She can get stuffed," snarled Agatha. "Oh, poor Phil. What if it's brain damage?"

"Here comes the surgeon now," said Bill.

"Mr. Marshall has suffered a concussion," he said. "He must have a very strong head. There is no sign of brain damage."

"I would like to try to have a word with him," said Bill.

"Make it short. He'll need a lot of rest."

Agatha made to follow Bill. The surgeon barred her way. "Who are you?"

"His boss."

"Then I cannot allow you to go in. I have to allow the police, but after that only family will be allowed in to see him."

Deaf to Agatha's protests, he led Bill away.

"Oh, God," prayed Agatha. "Let him be all right."

"Didn't think you believed in God," said Charles.

"It's just an expression," said Agatha. "I think I'm an atheist."

"Do you know the definition of an atheist?"

"No."

"An atheist," said Charles, "is someone without any invisible means of support."

"Oh, ha bloody ha."

Bill was gone only ten minutes. "He's very weak," he said. "But he told me that according to Doris Crampton, everyone seemed to know that Fred often nicked a bottle of wine. I'm going back to pull her in for impeding the police in their inquiries. Agatha, pull your staff off the case for at least a week because we will now be doing door-to-door inquiries in that hellhole of a village."

"Are you going to obey him?" asked Charles as Agatha drove them back to her cottage.

"I do think I'll leave it all alone for a few days. Alison had nothing of any interest to tell me. Besides, the place is crawling with press."

"I might trot along there tomorrow and blend with the locals."

"You!"

"I'll go in disguise."

"Remember the Crampton sisters have had a look at you. And that posh accent of yours will give you away."

"I'll have you know I can talk mangel-wurzel with the best of them."

"Charles, look what happened to Phil. I don't want anything like that happening to you."

"Dear me. Our Aggie actually has a heart!"

Charles, wearing some of his undergardener's clothes and a flat cap, and with his face and hands stained brown and a straggly moustache pasted to his upper lip, arrived in Lower Tapor at lunchtime the following day.

The pub was quite full when he entered. Silence fell as everyone turned to survey the newcomer.

Charles made his way to the bar. "Pint o' Hook Norton," he ordered. There was no sign of Paul Chambers. His pint was pulled for him by the gypsy-looking Elsie.

Charles turned round and saw a small table with one chair over by the window. He took his pint over and sat down. He took out a packet of tobacco and rolled himself a cigarette. And waited.

He guessed that curiosity would soon get the better of the locals.

Sure enough, after five minutes a heavyset man came up and loomed over him.

"You're a stranger here."

Charles nodded.

"What you doin' here?"

"Mind yer own bizzness," said Charles.

This seemed to be a satisfactory reply. Charles had guessed that any sign of friendliness would be treated with suspicion.

The man pulled up a chair and joined him. "Had an accident, then?" he asked, nodding in the direction of Charles's hands. Charles had bandaged his hands to disguise the fact that they had never done any hard work at all.

"Yus."

"Terrible goin's-on in this village," said the man.

Charles looked indifferent. "Yes, murders, that's what we're having. And it was them up at the manor that did it."

"Why you say that, then?" asked Charles.

"Cos they did. Wanted the old woman's money. Then Fred, he was the gardener, he got wise to them so they killed him as well."

Charles decided it was time to show some animation. "Reckon you must all be scared."

"Naw, they won't touch one o' us provided we keep our mouths shut. We got ways to protect ourselves."

"Like what?" asked Charles.

"Keith!" shouted Elsie from behind the bar. "You get right over here."

Charles's companion got reluctantly to his feet. Elsie leaned over the bar and hissed something at him. He left the pub quickly.

Deciding there wouldn't be much more to be found, Charles left. But he wondered about those ways of protection. Witchcraft?

Toni felt excited as she dressed in dark clothes on Saturday evening and then waited for George.

She was sure they wouldn't find anything, but the outing would make her feel like a real detective, stalking and hiding in the bushes.

George arrived on time. "This is my new flat," said Toni proudly.

"Where did you get the furniture?" asked George.

"Agatha bought it from the owner."

George looked at the battered sofa and scuffed chairs. "You could do better. I've got some bits and pieces in the attic. You could come over one day and have a look."

"That's very kind of you."

"So let's go on the witch hunt. I've been there already and I've found a good place where we can hide out and see what goes on at the top of that hill—if anything."

There was a glade at the top of the hill surrounded by trees. They hid in the bushes at the side. A full moon rose overhead.

Toni wanted to pass the time chatting but he whispered to

her to be quiet because sounds in the countryside at night could carry very far.

By eleven-thirty, Toni was beginning to feel cramped and bored. Then they heard voices. Soon they heard people approaching up the hill.

Toni peered through the bushes and stifled a gasp. Paul Chambers was leading a small group of villagers into the grove. Elsie, the barmaid, was beside him.

At first it looked as if they had all come up for a picnic. Sandwiches and bottles were passed around. Then, just before midnight, Paul said, "It's time."

They all began to undress until they were stark naked. A CD of some oriental music began to play. They all joined hands in a circle and began to dance. Paul had a good figure but the rest had sagging rolls of white fat. Flaccid breasts jiggled, sagging buttocks rolled. Toni could feel laughter bubbling up inside her. She pressed a hand to her mouth. At last she could not contain herself any longer and let out a burst of laughter.

"That's torn it," said George. He grabbed her hand. "Crouch down and run."

Doubled up, they raced through the undergrowth until George pulled up short. "Wrong way," he said. They were standing on the lip of a disused quarry. "Back into those bushes over there and hope they don't find us," said George.

They lay down flat under the bushes. Toni felt the beating of her heart was so loud that the pursuers must surely hear it.

Then they heard Chambers's voice. "I'll swear they came this way," and Elsie's reply, "Probably kids."

In the clear moonlight, George could see Paul and Elsie standing on the lip of the quarry. Both were still naked.

"Forget about them, darlin'," said Elsie. "Let's have some fun."

"Leave me alone, you silly tart. This is serious."

"What did you call me?"

"I said you were a silly tart and that's all you are."

"You said you'd marry me."

"Oh, not again. The things I say in bed. Forget it."

In front of Toni's and George's horrified eyes, Elsie gave Paul an enormous push in his back and he stumbled forward and fell over the quarry. He screamed as he went down and then there was no sound at all.

Elsie peered over the quarry and then turned and ran away.

George could feel Toni shaking and put an arm around her. "Hold on," he said. "I'll get the police."

Agatha was awakened the following morning by the shrill, insistent clamour of her doorbell.

She glanced at her bedside clock. Six in the morning!

She struggled out of bed, wrapped herself in a dressing gown and went downstairs. Agatha opened the door and found a white-faced Toni and a tall man she did not recognize.

"It's terrible," said Toni. "Paul Chambers has been murdered."

"Come in," said Agatha. And to George, "Who are you?"

"I'm George Pyson, the factor for Mrs. Tamworthy's estate."

She led them into the kitchen. "Sit down. Toni, what's been going on?"

Toni turned to George. "You tell her."

So George told the tale of the witch-hunt and then how

134

Elsie had shoved Paul into the quarry. "He broke his neck in the fall," he ended.

"Toni," said Agatha, "you should have told me about this."

"We didn't have any hard facts," said George. "We just went on the off chance."

Agatha's eyes were suddenly hard. She surveyed George. "How old are you?"

"I am thirty-three and no, I do not have designs on your young detective."

"We're friends," said Toni, and George smiled at her.

"I'll make us coffee," said Agatha. "I don't suppose either of you have had any sleep."

"No," said Toni. She stifled a yawn. "That Collins woman interviewed me all night."

"The good thing is," said Agatha over her shoulder as she plugged in the percolator, "you won't have to turn up in court for Paul Chambers's trial. The bad thing is that Lower Tapor will now be crammed with the world's press. Murder *and* witchcraft in an English village! Toni, you'd better rest up today. That should keep you out of harm's way."

At that moment, Charles ambled into the kitchen. Agatha told him about the latest murder.

"Chambers is no great loss," said Charles callously. "Good for you, Toni."

"I feel it's all my fault," said Toni. "It was when I saw them all dancing around naked that I began to laugh. All that loose white fat jiggling about. That's why we ran to the quarry and hid in the bushes and that's why Paul and Elsie followed us there."

Agatha scowled into her coffee cup. She could feel a treacherous roll of fat at her midriff. Oh, to be as young as Toni.

"With all the press that are going to be around," she said, "we'd all better keep clear of the manor until the fuss dies down. But I hate to leave it alone."

"I wonder if Mrs. Tamworthy made any enemies in her past," said George. "I mean, look at the way she treated her own children. Maybe there's someone she crossed before."

Agatha brightened. "That's a good idea." Then she suddenly looked full at George, said a hurried "Excuse me" and rushed up the stairs.

"Gone to grout her face," said Charles.

Sure enough, Agatha reappeared fifteen minutes later with her face made up.

Toni gave a massive yawn and knuckled her eyes.

"Come on, young lady," said George. "Time I got you home."

When they had left, Charles helped himself to one of Agatha's cigarettes. "What goes on there?" he asked.

"Nothing. He's too old for her."

"And too young for you," murmured Charles.

"I'm going back to sleep," said Agatha. She had been roused from a glorious dream of Christmas, complete with James smiling down at her, and she wanted to see if she could recapture it.

"Now you've got to take all that make-up off again," Charles called after her.

But Agatha pretended not to hear.

George drove Toni to her flat. He turned to her and said, "Get some sleep and don't answer the phone or the doorbell. If the police want to interview either of us again, they can just wait until Monday morning."

Toni thanked him and then hesitated, waiting for him to say something else. But he climbed out and went round and held the car door open for her.

"Bye," said Toni and went inside.

In her flat she undressed, took a shower and climbed into her narrow bed. He hadn't said anything about seeing her again. Maybe she wasn't posh enough. It wasn't as if she was romantically interested in him. He was too old.

She slept all day and awoke feeling refreshed, but wondering if she would get any more sleep that night. Toni decided to drop in at the Tammy Club. It seemed ages since she had gone clubbing and she wanted to be among people her own age.

There had been protests about the club being open on Sundays, but somehow it managed to survive the complaints.

Toni entered and breathed in the old familiar smell of alcohol and pot. Strobe lights were flashing across the floor where dancers gyrated to the loud beat of the music.

"Hi! Look, folks, it's Tone," called a girl.

Toni was soon surrounded by some of her ex–school friends. One of them, Karen, shouted above the music, "Heard you was a tec."

Toni nodded in reply. The music suddenly finished and the DJ said, "Taking five minutes out, folks."

"Let's get a drink," said Karen.

They all moved to the bar. They pressed Toni to talk about her work, but Toni did not feel like going into details. "What's the talent like?" she asked.

A thin spotty girl called Laura said, "You haven't met the latest dreamboat. His name's Rex."

"Sounds like a dog or a cinema," said Toni.

"Look, that's him over there." Laura pointed to where a young man was slouched at the end of the bar. He was wearing a black leather jacket over his bare chest and leather trousers. His black hair was gelled into spikes. He had a stud below his bottom lip. His face was very white and he had heavy black eyebrows and designer stubble.

Toni suddenly felt a wave of isolation. Not so long ago, she might have found Rex attractive. But not now. She listened to the chatter of her former friends and felt she was looking at them through the wrong end of a telescope. The music started up again.

"Gotta go," muttered Toni and headed towards the door and out into the night. She took great gulps of fresh air. Maybe after a week or two, she would go back to the club, but at the moment she felt caught somewhere between the youth of her former school friends and what she thought of as the "old folks" at the detective agency.

Agatha kept clear of the manor house for a week. She knew it would be impossible to move freely with press and police swarming all over the place. Other cases had to be dealt with. She missed Toni, who was taking driving lessons, interrupted by police interviews.

After work she prowled the supermarkets because they were already selling Christmas decorations, wondering which ones would look best. She ordered a turkey from a Norfolk farm, to be delivered ten days before Christmas. She ordered a new cooker with an oven large enough for the bird to fit into.

Charles had disappeared back to his home, promising to return the following week.

On Friday evening Bill Wong called on her at her cottage. He looked tired. "We're getting nowhere. Elsie has been arrested, of course, but nothing about the murder at the manor or who killed that poor old man."

"This factor, George Pyson," said Agatha, "anything odd about him?"

"Highly respectable, by all accounts."

"Married?"

"He was, but his wife died of cancer five years ago. No children. Why are you interested in him?"

"I think he's interested in young Toni and he's too old for her."

"I sat in on the interviews with Toni. I would say that young lady is older than her years. Very sensible. I wouldn't worry about her."

"You've interviewed all of them at the manor house," said Agatha. "Can you think of any one of them that might have done it?"

"I've thought and thought. And the more I think about it, I'm amazed that with such a mother they've all turned out sane. Now, the people in the village with their damned witchcraft, it's beginning to seem more and more likely that one or several of them might have conspired to murder her."

"I can't see them doing that," said Agatha.

"Why?"

"She charged them low rents. With her gone, ten to one the

family or whoever they sell the estate to will jack up the rents. Where was Mrs. Tamworthy brought up?"

"I don't know. You'll need to ask one of the family. Why?"

"Maybe it was someone out of her past."

"If you find out anything, let me know."

On Saturday evening Toni was walking along the street to her flat, elated at having got her driving licence, when she felt her arm seized. She swung round. Her brother's beery face was thrust into her own. "You're coming home, now," he said.

"Leave me alone," howled Toni. People scurried past them, averting their eyes. No one wanted to get involved. These days, villains were apt to sue the rescuer for assault.

Toni kicked and struggled but Terry was much stronger. A battered Land Rover came along the street and stopped abruptly. George Pyson jumped down.

"Leave her alone this minute," he shouted at Terry.

"Piss off, you posh git," snarled Terry. "This here's a family matter."

George seized Terry's arm and twisted it up his back. Terry howled in pain.

"Who is this?" asked George.

"My brother," gasped Toni, breaking free. "He's trying to get me to go home and I don't want ever to go there again."

"Are you going to go quietly?" asked George, giving Terry's arm a painful wrench.

"You're breaking me arm! Yes. Let me go."

George released him and Terry ran off down the street.

Toni said in a low voice, "Thanks." He won't want to know me now, she thought, coming from my sort of family.

But George said, "Let's go for a drink. I only caught glimpses of you at police headquarters when I was being grilled in one room and you in another. I'd better move the car. It's blocking the street." A volley of horns bore witness to this.

They both climbed into the Land Rover and George drove off.

"I'll just park in the square and we'll go to the nearest pub and you can tell me about your driving lessons."

"I passed today," said Toni. "I'm still a bag of nerves."

In the pub he asked her to tell him why she had left home and listened while Toni recounted how Agatha had come to her rescue.

"And your mother?" he asked. "Any chance of getting her into a rehab?"

"Rehabs cost a lot of money."

"They take a few National Health patients. Her doctor could put her name down. She may have to wait but it would be better than nothing."

"She's hardly ever sober enough to listen to me. Maybe I'll try when Terry's not around."

Toni eyed him covertly, wondering whether he was coming on to her, but after she had finished her drink, he said briskly, "Right, young lady, let's get you home."

And that is exactly what he did, giving her a cheery goodbye as she climbed down from the Land Rover.

As she watched him drive off, her mobile phone rang. It was Agatha. "I passed my test," said Toni.

"Great. We'll get you some old banger. I'll pick you up tomorrow."

"Back to the village?" asked Toni uneasily.

"No, we're going to find out more about Phyllis Tamworthy."

NINE

✝

ALISON HAD informed Agatha that her mother had been brought up in the village of Pirdey in Lancashire. With Toni studying a route map beside her, Agatha drove northwards out of the Cotswolds.

Rain smeared the windscreen and she switched on the wipers. A blustery wind was pulling ragged grey clouds across a large sky. Out on the motorway, spray from huge lorries made driving a misery. Agatha wished Charles had not turned down her invitation to come with them. In his company she often stopped thinking about James Lacey. Also, she liked being accompanied by a man after years of battling on her own. She sometimes felt it was still an old-fashioned world. A woman on her own was often treated by hoteliers and waiters like a second-class citizen.

She had been pleased to learn that Phyllis Tamworthy had been brought up in a village. If she had been brought up in a

large city, there would be little chance of anyone remember-
ing her, thought Agatha, forgetting that anyone who remembered Phyllis would have to be pretty old. Phyllis's maiden
name had been Wright. Agatha wished it had been something
more unusual.

They stopped off at a motorway restaurant to break their
journey. Toni had recently read an article which stated that the
diet of the working classes was still abysmal, consisting as it
did of mircrowaveable meals and take-out food. But Agatha
was tucking into a large plate of greasy eggs and bacon with
every sign of enjoyment.

Soon they were on their way again. Agatha slid a CD into
the player and the strains of a Brahms symphony filled the
car. Toni did not like classical music but was trying hard.

Toni had expected the village to be like Carsely but it was a
grim little place stuck out on moorland. The rain had stopped
but a yellow watery sunlight only enhanced the drabness of the
place, which seemed to consist of one long straggling street.
Agatha drew up outside a sub–post office and general stores.
"Wait here," she said to Toni. She marched in and asked an
Asian woman behind the counter where she could find some
old residents.

The woman, her sari a bright splash of colour in the dingy
shop, volunteered the information that the elderly residents
met in the community centre at the eastern end of the village
in half an hour for tea.

Agatha rejoined Toni in the car. "We need to wait for half
an hour. The old folks meet up at the community centre. The
woman in there says it's at the eastern end of the village."

"What's the eastern end?" asked Toni.

Agatha scowled horribly. Then she admitted, "Blessed if I

know." She got out and went back into the shop, returning after a few minutes to say, "It's along on the left. We may as well wait outside until they all turn up."

The community centre was in what had once been a villa. A pokerwork sign with the legend THE HEIGHTS swung in the wind.

"I wonder why they call it that?" mused Toni. "The countryside around here is as flat as a pancake."

"Who cares?" snapped Agatha and Toni gave her a hurt look of surprise.

The fact was that Agatha was uncomfortable in Toni's company, the glowing youth of the young girl making her feel ancient.

To make matters worse, when the elderly began to arrive and Agatha made to get out of the car, she stifled a groan and clutched her hip. "I'll help you out," said Toni.

"Leave me alone," howled Agatha.

She rubbed her hip furiously while she watched the old folks totter up the short drive to the centre.

"Is something up with your hip?" asked Toni nervously.

"There is nothing up with me," raged Agatha. "It was that long drive."

"I can do some of the driving," said Toni. "I got my licence first time off."

"I may let you." Toni as a novice driver might give Agatha something to feel superior about.

When they entered the community centre, a stout matron was ushering men and women—mostly women—to seats at a long table where cakes and sandwiches had been laid out.

Agatha approached her. "I am a private detective," she

said. "I am investigating the death of Phyllis Tamworthy, whose name when she was brought up in this village was Phyllis Wright."

"I think you should wait until they have had their tea," said the woman. "For some of them it's the only food they get. Pensions don't go far these days. I'm Gladys."

"I'm Agatha and this is Toni."

"If you and your daughter would like to sit over in the corner, I'll ask them when they've settled down."

"She's not my . . ." began Agatha, but Gladys had walked away.

Agatha watched the elderly ladies. She watched the wrinkled hands, some of them trembling as they reached for sandwiches. Is this what we all must come to? she wondered sadly.

Toni covertly watched Agatha. Had she offended her in some way? She owed Agatha so much. Gratitude *did* weigh heavily, like a physical load.

"I'm sorry," said Agatha suddenly. "I'm feeling a bit off-colour. I think if we find anything worthwhile here, we'll check into a hotel somewhere."

Toni was about to say she would not mind driving back but stopped herself. She had a feeling that the ferociously independent Agatha Raisin wouldn't like that suggestion.

There was very little conversation amongst the elderly. For long periods, the only sounds were the clinking of cups and the chewing of jaws.

At last Gladys strode into the centre of the room. "Ladies and gentlemen," she said, "these ladies want to know if anyone remembers . . . who was it?"

"Phyllis Wright," said Agatha.

There was a gentle murmuring and then a very old lady croaked out. "I 'member her. She were at t'school same time as me."

Another one said, "War she the fatty in Miss Gilchrist's class?"

"Aye, that be her," said the first woman. "Teacher's pet. Allus sucking up to teacher and putting on airs but she warn't nobody."

"I don't suppose Miss Gilchrist is still alive," said Agatha.

"Her died . . . when was it?" said the first woman.

"Right after her gave Phyllis a right bollocking. Said her had cheated."

"What did she die of?" asked Agatha.

"What's your name?"

"Agatha."

"I'm Elsie and this here is Rose. Her died o' a heart attack and her so young. Course she seemed old to us then but she was about thirty or so."

"When did Phyllis leave the village?"

Elsie sighed. "Good thing you're asking us about them old days. Can't right remember yesterday, but the old days are as dear as clear. Let me see. Her was working over at Bessops Factory. Sauce makers they were. Now Hugh Tamworthy, he war a brickie and he war engaged to Carrie Shufflebottom. Then he won the lottery. Next thing we know, Phyllis had got her hands on him and they disappeared for a bit and came back married. The brickworks over at Rumton was going under and Hugh bought it. They took a bungalow out o' the village in the country cos no one in the village would speak to them cos o' Carrie."

"Where is Carrie now?" asked Agatha.

"You'll find her at Sun Cottage, right at the end. Go back past the post office and out that way. The last one you come to."

Outside, Toni said, "Phyllis is beginning to sound like one copper-bottomed bitch."

"Let's hope this Carrie has all her marbles," said Agatha. "Seems a shame. Those two we were talking to must be the same age as Phyllis was and yet Phyllis seemed pretty hale and hearty. Oh, God," said Agatha passionately, "I hope I don't end up like those poor old souls."

Sun Cottage belied its name. It faced north and was built of red brick, still sooty from the days of coal.

"I wonder if Carrie ever married?" Agatha pushed open a rickety wooden gate and led the way through a small weedy front garden. She rang the bell. A dingy lace curtain at a window to the right of the door twitched. Then the door opened.

Carrie Shufflebottom was proof that even the tremendously obese can live to old age. She was a massive woman with a large round rosy face and faded blue eyes. Her iron-grey hair was still thick.

"What?" she demanded.

Agatha patiently explained what they were doing and what they wanted to know.

"You'd best come in," she said, turning away, her large hips brushing against each wall of a narrow passage.

They followed her into a dark front parlour. The room was cold and sparsely furnished. Carrie sank down into a large battered armchair. Agatha and Toni sat on an equally battered sofa. A canary in a cage by the window chirped dismally and a rising wind moaned in the chimney. A grandfather clock in the corner gave a genteel cough before chiming out the hour.

"I'm not offering you tea," said Carrie. "I've just had mine." Cake crumbs were strewn across her bosom. She was wearing a man's shirt and tracksuit bottoms and trainers.

"So you want to know if anyone from around here might have wanted to murder Phyllis?" said Carrie. Her voice was surprisingly light and pleasant and not marred by the strong local accent of the villagers they had met. "I could have murdered her myself. Hugh Tamworthy was a good man. But innocent. The minute he won that lottery money, she threw herself at him. She made my life a misery when we were both at school, poking fun at my name. I only saw Hugh one more time after his wedding. About two years after they were married he called round here, right out of the blue. He was that upset. I hoped for one mad moment that he'd come back to me." She gave a wry smile. "Men can be so insensitive. He came to tell me he'd fallen in love with a girl who worked in the office at the brickworks. He said he was going to ask Phyllis for a divorce. He said Phyllis didn't want children and he'd always wanted children. The girl's name was Susan Mason. I'm afraid I lost my temper and told him to get out. I said he'd jilted me and hurt me badly."

"But he didn't divorce Phyllis," said Agatha.

"I heard later two things had happened. Phyllis was pregnant with her first child and Susan had disappeared. She left the office one night and no one saw her again. The search went on and on but they never found her. Phyllis had a hell of a temper. She probably threatened the girl. Soon afterwards, they sold the brickworks and bought another one down south somewhere."

"Did you ever marry?" asked Toni.

"I decided to get an education. I went to university and ended up teaching at the village school until the government closed it down. Not a very adventurous life. No, I never married."

"Are any of Susan's family still alive?"

"There's a younger sister over in Stoke. Wanda. She married quite well. Married an accountant. What was his name? I know. Mark Nicholson. Hand me that phone book over there."

"Over there" was the floor under the table. Toni handed her the phone book and she riffled through the pages. "Here we are. This must be him. Take a note." Agatha fished a notebook out of her handbag. "Mark Nicholson, 5, Cherry Tree Close, Stafford Road, Stoke-on-Trent."

Toni drove Agatha in the direction of Stoke. Agatha, feeling the pain in her hip was getting worse, let her take over. To Agatha's irritation, Toni drove easily and well. "We'd better stop somewhere and get a street map," said Agatha. "There's a newsagent's."

Toni parked neatly between two cars. Agatha scowled. She herself still needed the length of a truck to park properly.

Toni darted into the shop and came out brandishing a street map. "Let me have it," ordered Agatha, who was hating not being in control. She studied it and then said, "We're in luck. It's on this side of Stoke. Go straight ahead through three roundabouts and turn sharp left at the fourth. That's Stafford Road. Cherry Tree Close is the third on the left."

The close was one of those builders' developments where an effort had been made to make every house look different and yet the final result was that they all looked the same. They were two-storied houses built of grey stone. The uniform-sized windows gazed blankly out over small neat gardens. "Isn't it odd that Phyllis never mentioned having had a previous brickworks?" said Agatha.

"Maybe ashamed of herself for having ruined Carrie's engagement and frightened off Susan."

"I wonder. There's number 5. Let's hope someone's at home."

Toni rang the bell. They waited and waited but there was no reply. "Let's get back to the car and wait," said Agatha.

"She might be at work," remarked Toni.

"Maybe not. She would be near to Phyllis's age. So she would probably be retired." Agatha lit a cigarette. "I wonder if it'll snow this Christmas."

"Can you remember a white Christmas?" asked Toni.

"Not one. This global warming would just come along when nobody wants it," complained Agatha.

Toni repressed a smile. The scientists were worried about global warming, governments were worried about it, but Agatha Raisin was fed up because she wouldn't have a white Christmas. She said, "Never mind. It's usually dark and dreary in December and if you have a tree and a lot of lights and decorations, it'll look very pretty."

"I've an awful lot of people to invite," said Agatha. "I don't think my dining room will hold them all."

"Is there a hall in the village?"

"Yes, but it's pretty dingy."

"Still, you could decorate it and hide the dinginess. Or maybe you could get extra tables and put them together so that they ran from the dining room across the hall and into the living room," said Toni.

Agatha brightened. "Now, that might work. A lot of the ladies' society were fed up because I didn't invite them to the last one."

"Someone's coming," said Toni. "A car's coming along."

A new Audi moved past them and drove up and into the garage at the side of number 5.

"Good," said Agatha. "Let's go."

The woman getting out of her car looked at them curiously. She was slim and well preserved with dyed blonde hair, large, slightly protruding hazel eyes, a small mouth, and a long thin nose. A Hermès scarf was tied tightly round her neck. Agatha judged her to be in her seventies and that she had had some plastic surgery.

Agatha went up to her and explained who they were and why they were there.

"I don't know that I can help you," said Wanda. "I mean, what can you do after all these years? The police searched everywhere."

"Did they interview Phyllis Tamworthy?"

"Oh, yes. Over and over again. Hugh Tamworthy was going to get a divorce and marry my sister. I think Phyllis frightened her into running away. But she didn't take any of her clothes or her passport."

"Did you read in the newspapers that Phyllis was murdered?"

"Yes, and I was glad to hear someone had at last got the guts to bump the horrible woman off."

"Do you know where the Tamworthys lived when they were up here?" asked Toni.

"They had a bungalow in Rumton."

"Where exactly?" asked Toni eagerly.

Agatha looked at her in surprise.

"I'm sure it was at Rumton near the old brickworks. They're closed down now and it's a nursery and garden furniture place."

Agatha longed to ask Wanda where she was on the day that Phyllis was murdered but knew that only the police could really go around asking questions like that.

Instead she asked, "Can you think of anyone from Phyllis's past who might have wanted to kill her?"

"Carrie Shufflebottom hated Phyllis for taking Hugh away. She was engaged to him. But she was always a gentle soul."

Back in the car, Agatha rounded on Toni. "Why did you want to know where that bungalow was?"

Toni's eyes shone with excitement. "Don't you see? Phyllis may have bumped her off."

"We're looking for who killed Phyllis, not who Phyllis killed."

"But if she was a murderess, then that would be even more motive for someone to kill her."

"Oh, very well," said Agatha sulkily.

They found the bungalow by asking at the nursery. An old lady answered the door to them. Is everyone around here ancient? thought Agatha. Will we all end up in Carsely supporting ourselves on our Zimmer frames? She explained who they were and why they were visiting.

"I remember Phyllis and Susan," said the old lady. "I'm Pearl Dawson. Come in."

They went into a cluttered parlour, redolent of old body,

peppermints and pine disinfectant. Mrs. Dawson seemed to be crippled with arthritis. She winced as she lowered herself into a chair. "I need two hip replacements." She sighed. "But I've been waiting two and a half years now." As if to mock her, a voice from a small television set in the corner: "Today the government said that the National Health Service has cut waiting lists dramatically."

"Oh, turn that thing off," said Pearl. "Nothing but lies."

She was very thin and very wrinkled, with pink scalp showing through strands of grey hair.

"Now, what can I tell you?" she went on. "I mind Susan. Such a pretty, jolly girl. Something bad happened to her. She'd never have run away."

Toni said bluntly, "Do you think Phyllis might have killed her?"

Pearl looked shocked. "Never even crossed my mind."

"Let's just suppose," said Toni eagerly, "that Phyllis was sweet to Susan and offered her a lift home. Did you hear if there was anyone else around when she left the office?"

"I heard she was working late," said Pearl. "The gossips said she often worked late, and Hugh Tamworthy as well. But he didn't that night. Phyllis had sent him into Stoke to pick up some curtain material she had chosen. It was late-night shopping there. Maybe Susan was waiting for him to call back. Some of the brickies said she was in love with Hugh."

"So," said Toni excitedly, "Phyllis kills her. She's got to get rid of the body. Is there anywhere round about here where one could hide a body?"

Pearl smiled. "You do have a good imagination, young lady. There's the garden, but nothing's been done to that for ages. There's an old well but the police searched that."

Agatha began to get interested. If the police had been searching around the bungalow, they must have wondered about Phyllis.

"Anywhere else?" she asked.

Can't think of anywhere. There's the old privy out back. No one could take it down because it's listed as being of historical importance. Imagine! An old Victorian toilet being of interest to anyone."

"Do you mind if we have a look?" asked Agatha.

"Suit yourself. It's up at the end of the back garden. If you don't mind, I'll stay here. It hurts to move."

"What is the name of your member of parliament?" asked Agatha.

"Mr. Wither. Why?"

"Have you thought of phoning him to complain about not getting your hip replacements?"

"I couldn't do that!"

"Well, I could," said Agatha truculently. "Where's the phone book? The House isn't sitting at the moment, so he should be at home."

Agatha was full of surprises, thought Toni as she listened to Agatha Raisin in full bullying mode berating the member of parliament.

When she at last put down the phone, she grinned and said, "Good. That's settled. He's getting on to the hospital right away. I'll phone you next week and make sure someone is doing something about it. You must remember that she who screams the loudest gets the best service."

As Pearl stammered out her thanks, they headed out of the house and round to the weedy overgrown garden at the back.

"Just look at that!" said Agatha in disgust, pointing to the privy at the end of the garden. "It's practically fallen down. The council will stop anyone from getting rid of the dreadful thing and yet they won't do anything to keep it repaired."

They stumbled through weeds and tussocks of grass. The wooden door of the privy was hanging on its hinges. Agatha jerked it open and then jumped back as the rusty hinges snapped and the door fell into the garden.

"It was about to fall off anyway," she said. They peered inside. The toilet itself had been removed. Nothing but an earthen floor and a few rusting garden implements showing it had once been used as a garden shed.

"So, now, Miss Bright Ideas," said Agatha, "do we dig up the floor?"

"What else?" said Toni cheerfully. "There's a spade over there that looks as if it might still stand the strain."

"I think you're wasting your time. I saw a garden seat among the weeds. I'm going there for a smoke. It's all yours."

Toni started to dig and then stopped as she heard a scream from the garden.

She ran out. Agatha had sat down on a rotting wooden garden chair which had collapsed under her, tumbling her onto the grass.

Toni helped her up, trying not to laugh.

"Snakes and bastards," howled Agatha. "The grass is wet. Oh, get on with it, Toni, and I'll sit on the back step at the kitchen door."

Toni went back to digging. The earth was hard-packed. Once she got through the surface layer, the going became easier. She persevered, sweat running down her face. She stopped for a moment and looked out the door. Agatha was sitting, blowing smoke up into the grey sky, a dreamy look on her face.

Probably dreaming of a white Christmas, thought Toni and went back to work. But as her arms began to ache, she felt foolish. What a stupid, wild idea. She went out and called to Agatha that she was going to fill the hole in again. As she turned round, a shaft of sunlight cut through the clouds and shone straight into the hole in the privy. There was a small knob of something yellowish-white showing through the earth at the bottom of the hole. Heart beating hard, Tonie lay down on the floor and began to scrape the earth away with her fingers. The top of what looked like a skull was gradually exposed.

Toni got slowly to her feet. Her knees were trembling.

"Agatha!" she called. "I've found something."

Agatha and Toni met up several hours later in the reception area of Stoke police station. "Are you psychic or something?" grumbled Agatha. "Got gypsy blood? How did you guess Phyllis might have killed Susan?"

"It seemed logical," said Toni. "I mean, who else would have wanted to get rid of her?"

"Oh, well, I suppose we'd better find somewhere to stay the night," said Agatha, stifling a yawn.

"The detectives who interviewed me said we could go back home," said Toni. "Just so long as we report to Mircester tomorrow. I don't mind driving."

"All right. I want to see if my cats are all right."

As Toni drove steadily down the motorways, Agatha kept glancing over at her. This is how Samson must have felt when his hair was cut, she thought. Toni's a terrific asset but she does make me feel old and dithering. And I am not old! Today's fifties are yesterdays forties, or so they say.

She wanted to assert herself by taking over the driving, but her eyelids began to droop and soon she was fast asleep.

"Wake up. You're home!" Toni's voice roused her up from the depths. Agatha rubbed her eyes. "Can't be. I can't have been asleep all that time."

"You obviously needed it," said Toni cheerfully. "If you call me a taxi, I'll get home myself."

Agatha was about to suggest that Toni stay the night at her place but then realized the girl would probably like to get to her own place for a change of clothes in the morning.

"Come inside," she said, "and I'll phone for a cab."

Agatha's cats came purring up to meet her. She looked at her watch. Three in the morning! Her stomach rumbled. She wondered whether she should offer Toni any food but was suddenly desperate to get rid of her. Agatha telephoned for a taxi, told Toni it would take twenty minutes, and went upstairs to the bathroom.

She paused on the landing. The faint sounds of snoring were coming from the spare bedroom. She looked in through the open door. Charles was sprawled on his back, fast asleep.

Agatha, reluctant to go downstairs and join Toni, undressed, took a quick shower, put on a nightdress, slippers and a kimono, and then went back down to the kitchen.

Toni was fast asleep, her head on the kitchen table. Agatha made herself a cup of black coffee and lit a cigarette. The sign on the packet said, "You may injure others with passive smoking." "Screw you," muttered Agatha, but she went and opened the kitchen door.

The trouble is, she thought, I've always been a sort of one-woman band. I've always believed I was a clever detective, but I think now I've simply been lucky and now I've got someone luckier than me. Then she smiled. Finding a skeleton in a toilet would not be many people's idea of luck. But why had Toni leaped so quickly to the idea that Phyllis might have murdered Susan? I hope my mind isn't ageing, thought Agatha. Good, there's the taxi.

She shook Toni awake and the girl stumbled out sleepily to the cab. "Don't come in until noon," said Agatha, "and then we'll go to the police station together."

Agatha retreated to the kitchen, took a microwave curry out of the fridge and popped it into the microwave. She stared as it went round and round until it pinged. She ate it out of the container, then shooed the cats back in from the garden, shut the door and crawled off to bed. Oh, for a good night's sleep!

She was awakened, it seemed to her, ten minutes later by Charles shaking her. "The police are downstairs."

Agatha groaned. "What's the time?"

"Nine o'clock. What have you been up to now?"

"Let me get dressed. What police?"

"Bill Wong and Detective Inspector Wilkes."

"Buzz off and give them coffee or something."

Agatha dressed hurriedly and headed for the stairs. Then she realized she had forgotten to put make-up on. She scurried back to the bathroom and made her face up in front of a magnifying mirror. "Toni doesn't need make-up," she muttered. "Blast Toni."

Wilkes looked at Agatha sternly as she entered the kitchen. He had a sheaf of faxes in front of him on the kitchen table. "I'm very tired," complained Agatha. "Toni and I were interviewed for hours up at Stoke."

"But I am interested in the murder of Phyllis Tamworthy," said Wilkes sternly. "Detective Sergeant Wong, you are on duty here, so take that cat off your neck."

Bill sheepishly removed Hodge from his shoulders and Boswell from his lap. Agatha felt a little stab of pleasure that they had come to her first and not to Toni, quickly banished when Wilkes said, "We have already interviewed Miss Gilmour. She claims that she was suddenly struck with the idea that Phyllis Tamworthy might be a murderess and might have murdered Susan Mason."

"It did seem an odd flight of fancy at the time," said Agatha. "Charles, please get me a cup of coffee."

"But Miss Gilmour told me the idea came to her after the evidence you had collected."

"What evidence?" asked Agatha.

"Mrs. Tamworthy had ruthlessly taken Hugh away from his fiancée the minute he had that lottery win. Then there was something about her being teacher's pet at school, and then the teacher disliking her and subsequently dying."

"Oh, that evidence," said Agatha weakly. "Yes, we both began to decide that Phyllis was a much nastier person than we had even begun to imagine. That was why I encouraged my detective to go ahead and dig up that privy."

And then Wilkes said those words Agatha had been beginning to dread. "Let's begin at the beginning, Mrs. Raisin."

Agatha wearily described their trip to the north and told him about everyone they had spoken to and what they had said, right up until Toni found the skeleton.

"You see," she ended by saying, "I thought it might have something to do with Phyllis's past. When will you get the DNA result from the skeleton?"

"Don't think we'll need it," said Wilkes. "Susan Mason's handbag was down the hole with her with her bank book in it, fragments of clothing, and we'll match the dentistry done on the teeth today sometime. What makes you think Phyllis might be the culprit? What about Hugh Tamworthy?"

"If he was weak enough to let Phyllis bully him into marrying her, then I can't see him having the guts or the reason to bump off Susan, a girl he genuinely seems to have been in love with. Oh, and don't forget that when she was at school, Phyllis fell out with her schoolteacher. Said schoolteacher died shortly afterwards."

"We'll look into that. I think it would be better if you kept well out of it from now on, Mrs. Raisin."

"What!" screeched Agatha. "You wouldn't ever have found that skeleton if it hadn't been for a brilliant piece of deduction." Agatha became aware that Charles was looking at her cynically ". . . by Toni," she added. "Besides, I'm being employed by the family."

"All right. Confine your investigations to the family and to whoever murdered Mrs. Tamworthy," said Wilkes. "But suspend your activities for a week or so and leave the police to do their job."

Agatha showed them out. The postman was just arriving. Agatha waited hopefully until he handed her a small pile of correspondence. She flicked through and found a highly coloured postcard of Tonga. She turned it over and read: "Working hard on the latest travel book. Will be back for Christmas. You'd love the sunshine here. Love, James."

She smiled with delight. She would make it a Christmas to remember.

Back in the kitchen, she put the postcard on the table and thumbed through the rest. "Junk mail and bills," she said.

"Who's the postcard from?"

"James."

"Aha. That explains the smile on your lips and the shine in your eyes. It's a dead duck, Aggie."

"Oh, shut up. I've got to get into the office, although I could do with some more sleep."

"Then go back to bed. You're the boss."

"No, I can't sleep now. I've got to get out to that blasted manor and see how they're all taking this latest development. Coming with me?"

"Why not?"

"I'd better get Doris to house-sit. The new cooker's arriving today."

"Cooker? Is this for Christmas? Decided to char another bird after all?"

"No, I'm not only getting a caterer, but a chef as well. I've ordered a decent turkey and I don't want to risk getting one of those nasty frozen supermarket ones if I leave it all to the caterers. I'll just phone Patrick and Phil as well and see how they are getting on and then we'll be off."

"How is Phil, by the way?"

"No bad effects after his lightning recovery. He's a tough old boy."

It was a steel-grey day as they drove towards the manor house. Flocks of migrating birds drew arrows across the sky. Coloured leaves spiralled down in front of the car. "It really is quite cold," said Agatha. "Perhaps it *will* snow this Christmas."

"It never snows at Christmas. You're building all this up to an unhealthy level."

"Nothing is going to go wrong."

"Except the final death of romance."

Agatha did not deign to reply as she turned into the gates of the manor.

"Can't see any police cars," said Charles.

"Maybe they've all gone off to their respective homes," said Agatha, "and the police are interviewing them there."

Jill, the groom, came round the side of the house as they were getting out of the car.

"Family at home?" asked Agatha.

"They're all at the funeral. They'll be back from the crematorium any minute now."

Agatha said, "I didn't know the body had been released for burial."

"Yes, about a week ago. I suppose it's all right if you go inside. Some women from the village are preparing sandwiches and things."

"I wonder if that's wise," said Charles as they walked into the manor. "Don't eat any sandwiches with green in them. Could be hemlock."

They could hear a clatter of plates coming from the kitchen. "Where will we wait?" asked Agatha. "I mean, it might look a bit cheeky to be found in the drawing room like guests."

"Particularly as it looks as if you've exposed dear mama as a murderess."

"I didn't think of that. They may not know. I mean, the police won't tell them anything until they have more proof. It's not as if any one of them were even born at the time. Phyllis was pregnant with the first one as far as I remember. I'm beginning to wonder what sort of man Hugh Tamworthy really was."

"Sick," said Charles laconically while he pushed open doors. "Look, there's a little room here."

"Used to be the morning room. We can wait here." Agatha followed him in. "What do you mean, sick?"

"Sick people gravitate to sick people. The formerly abused child marries a wife beater. The child of an alcoholic may not become one but ten to one will marry one. There are professional victims and martyrs all over the place . . . like you."

"Just what do you mean by that?" snarled Agatha.

"A normal person wouldn't have put up with James for a minute."

"I'll have you know, both my parents were alcoholics and I am not one, and neither is James. I could do with a drink right now, mind you."

"I hear them arriving." Charles walked to the window. "The men have black ties but the women are wearing their usual clothes. Just them, no one from the village except the ones in the kitchen and they're only here because they're being paid."

Agatha opened the door. "I'll waylay Alison. She isn't a member of the family except by marriage and she didn't like Phyllis."

She went out into the hall. Bert, Jimmy, Sadie, Fran and Sir Henry Field saw Agatha but simply walked past her into the drawing room. Alison came hurrying in after them and stopped short at the sight of Agatha.

"I'm surprised you should call at such a time," she said.

"You haven't heard?"

"Haven't heard what?"

"You'd better come into the morning room. There's been a new development."

Alison walked in, nodded to Sir Charles and demanded, "What?"

Agatha told her about finding the skeleton and the fact that Phyllis might have killed Susan.

Alison sat down and put her head in her hands. "This is awful," she mumbled.

"So this is the first you've heard of it?" asked Charles.

"Yes, I'd better tell the others. Wait here."

She got unsteadily to her feet. Charles put out an arm to help her but she gave him a weak smile. "I'll be all right."

She closed the door behind her.

"It's odd," said Agatha. "I'm actually beginning to feel sorry for the lot of them. What a mother! Let's hope it doesn't get round the village or we'll have all the press you can think of running around the place."

"Gosh," said Charles. He wrenched open the door. Two women from the village were standing across the hall, their ears pressed to the panel of the drawing room door. "What are you doing?" shouted Charles. "Get back to the kitchen!"

He turned to Agatha. "We'd better sit in the hall in case they come back. That's torn it. There's no use telling them not to talk and we've nothing to threaten them with."

Someone in the drawing room was sobbing. They waited and waited. A couple of times the kitchen door opened a crack and then closed again.

At last Alison came out. "They want you to leave. Jimmy looks on the point of breakdown. This is something I know nothing about. So I can't help you either. I really don't think you should be here on such a day. I'll call at your office if I have any news."

*   *   *

In the office, Mrs. Freedman said, "Phil came in. I sent him home. I hope you don't mind. I said it was too early."

"Poor man," exclaimed Agatha. "I'd better go and see him. What are Toni and Patrick doing?"

"Patrick's working on a divorce and Toni's out looking for a missing teenager."

"I've got things to do," said Charles. "I'll leave you to look after Phil. Drop me at your cottage and I'll pick up my car."

When Agatha arrived at Phil's cottage in Carsely, it was to find Mrs. Bloxby there.

"I just brought Mr. Marshall some of my chicken soup," said the vicar's wife.

"I haven't brought you anything, Phil," said Agatha. "But wait until you both hear the latest development. First, how are you, Phil?"

"I'm fine. I really would like to get back to work."

"Maybe tomorrow. Now listen to this . . ."

When she had finished the story of the skeleton, Mrs. Bloxby exclaimed in horror, "That woman was truly evil!"

"They'll have a devil of a job proving she did it after all this time, and with the case load the police have these days, they might not even try too hard. I mean, the murder was done either by Phyllis or Hugh or both of them. But Hugh was off on an errand for Phyllis, and—"

Her mobile phone rang. It was Doris Simpson. "Could you get back to the cottage? The men are here with the cooker but everything's got to be moved to fit it in."

"I'll be right there," said Agatha. She rang off. "Got to go."

When Agatha had left, Mrs. Bloxby said, "Agatha needs a psychiatrist."

"Mrs. Bloxby!"

"No, I don't mean for herself. I mean she should sit down with one of those police psychiatrists and tell him all she knows about Phyllis Tamworthy and her children."

"I might be able to help there," said Phil. "There's a retired psychiatrist who dealt with criminals. He lives in Bourton-on-the-Water. His name is Dr. Drayton. I hope he's still alive."

Agatha passed what she considered a wasted day. Anything to do with domesticity Agatha considered a wasted day. Electricians and plumbers had to be brought in to move the fridge and dishwasher and refit them to leave space for the large cooker. When everything was finished, the cooker sat there, squat, shiny and big, looking totally out of place.

When the men had finally gone, Agatha's phone rang. It was to be the first of many newspapers. The story had got out. How Agatha longed to take the credit for finding that skeleton and the only thing that stopped her was that Charles would lecture her and Toni would put her down as a jealous old bat.

Toni was in her flat having tea with George Pyson when Agatha rang her. George had just delivered one very comfortable leather armchair and a sturdy round pine table and had carried the ones those replaced down to his Land Rover, so Toni had made him tea.

"Toni," said Agatha, "get your glad rags on and full make-up and get to Carsely. The press will be here to interview you quite soon."

"Do I have to?" pleaded Toni. "You could handle it."

"They want you," said Agatha gruffly. "So hurry up."

Toni told George what had happened. He looked at her outfit critically. She was in her usual jeans and T-shirt.

"Have you got high heels and a skirt?"

"Yes."

"I'll wait in the car while you change. You don't need much make-up except lipstick and mascara."

Agatha opened the door to them an hour later and looked gloomily at Toni. The girl looked as if she had legs up to her armpits and with her eyelashes darkened, her eyes seemed even larger.

"The press, some of them, are in the sitting room."

Toni entered and blinked. Crammed into Agatha's sitting room were reporters, photographers and television cameramen.

Agatha listened sourly as Toni, falteringly at first, and then gaining confidence, told her story.

Then Toni was asked, "Why did you guess a body might be there? What made you leap to that conclusion?"

Toni smiled. "I work for Mrs. Agatha Raisin, who must be one of the most brilliant detectives in the country. She taught me everything I know. She encourages me to use my imagination. She could easily have said, 'Don't be silly,' but she said I was to go ahead."

God bless the girl, thought Agatha as the press began to demand photographs of them together.

When the session was finally over and Agatha was showing them out, she noticed George Pyson sitting in the Land Rover outside.

She turned and said to Toni, "What's he doing here?"

"He drove me over." For some reason Toni felt that it would not be wise to tell Agatha about the furniture. Agatha seemed to disapprove of George.

"Of course. You don't have a car," said Agatha. "We'll get one tomorrow. Invite George in and I'll open a bottle of wine."

Terry Gilmour watched his sister on television's late-night news. He felt bitter and mean with jealousy. The house was like a tip, strewn with bottles and cans and empty pizza cartons. His mother had suddenly appeared the day before. Shaky but stone cold sober, she had announced she was going to stay with an old school friend in Southampton who had managed to get off the booze and who was going to help her.

He began to cry drunkenly. He had no one to turn to. Even his friends were beginning to make excuses not to see him. He dimly remembered punching one of them in the face two nights before, but the rest of the evening was lost to him.

"I'll make them all sorry!" he shouted to the uncaring messy room.

Agatha studied George carefully and watched him closely when he talked to Toni, but she could detect no romantic interest there. A voice in her not usually overworked conscience was telling her that she was behaving like a jealous old maid.

The phone rang and she went to answer it. It was her young friend, Roy Silver.

"What's been going on?" he cried. "Finding a skeleton. You might have told me."

"As you can imagine, I'm busy. Press by the hordes."

"Press?" Roy was always trying to get himself some publicity. "Can I come down this weekend?"

"All right. But you might have to sleep on the sofa if Charles is using the spare room."

"See you."

George had got up to leave. "Do be careful," he said. "There's still a murderer out there."

After he had gone, taking Toni with him, Agatha received a phone call from Phil.

"Mrs. Bloxby had this great idea," said Phil. "She says what you need is a psychiatrist." Agatha felt a stab of hurt. "I'm surprised—" she was beginning furiously when Phil interrupted. "No, not for you. A retired police psychiatrist. We tell him everything we know about Phyllis and he might guess that there was something in her character which made her into a murderee."

"I don't need a shrink for that," said Agatha. "She murdered someone herself by the look of things, so it's easy to imagine someone wanted to kill her. In fact, there must be so many people who wanted to kill her; I don't know where to start."

"I've made an appointment for us," said Phil. "Of course, I can always cancel it."

"May as well give it a try," said Agatha. "Where? What time?"

"He lives in Bourton-on-the-Water. Ten tomorrow morning."

"Not far. I'll pick you up at half past nine."

Agatha yawned and stretched. Time for a good night's sleep. If only one hadn't got to eat the whole time. She was poking about in her freezer when the doorbell rang.

Probably Charles, she thought, and, not bothering to look through the spyhole, she swung the door open. Jimmy Tamworthy stood on the step, his face white, his eyes glittering. "I want a word with you," he hissed.

"It's late," said Agatha, barring the doorway. "Call on me at my office tomorrow."

"You'll hear me now, you bitch. How dare you go around saying my mother was a murderer! I could kill you."

"Another time," babbled Agatha. She nipped inside and slammed the door in his face. She crouched down in a chair in the kitchen while he rang the bell and hammered and kicked the door. Why amn't I phoning the police? she thought.

Why am I such a wimp?

She marched back to the door and shouted, "I've called the police!"

There was a sudden silence. Then a final kick at the door. A car door slammed and she peered through the spyhole and saw him driving off.

Agatha phoned Bill Wong at home, having to tell his formidable mother that it was a matter of life and death before she would call her son.

Bill listened carefully and said, "We should arrest him."

"I don't know. Could you maybe just give him a warning, Bill? I can't help thinking that if I had had a mother like Phyllis, I'd be off my trolley as well."

"All right. I'll speak to him tomorrow and put the fear of death into him. Hang on a minute. My mobile's ringing."

He seemed to be gone a long time. Then he finally came

back on the phone and said, "You'd better get over to Toni's flat. The police are on their way."

"What's happened?"

"That wretched brother of hers has hanged himself."

"Oh, God. I'll go immediately."

Agatha was gathering up her belongings, ready to leave, when she froze in horror. A key was turning in her front door. She ran into the kitchen and seized a carving knife.

When she returned to the hall, brandishing the knife, it was to find Charles smiling at her.

"Going to kill me, Aggie?"

"How did you get in?"

"I copied your keys."

"Snakes and bastards! How dare you? Oh, never mind. We've got to get to Toni's. Her brother has hanged himself."

When they arrived at Toni's flat, it was to find her being attended by a policewoman.

"Is there anything I can do?" asked Agatha.

Toni rose from the sofa where she had been sitting with her friend, Maggie, and flung her arms around Agatha and burst into tears.

"There, there," said Agatha, patting the girl awkwardly on the back. "We'll see you through this. Do you know where your mother is?"

Toni dried her tears. "She sent me a letter the other day. The police have contacted her. Her friend is driving her up from Southampton."

Agatha asked the policewoman, "Did he leave a note?"

"Fortunately he did. Trying to make everyone feel guilty."

"Will you need Miss Gilmour tonight? I'd like to take her home with me."

"I need to stay here for my mother," said Toni.

"Does she need to identify the body tonight?" Agatha asked the policewoman.

"No, tomorrow will do." She turned to Toni. "Are you sure you wouldn't like to let me phone for a doctor? He could give you something to make you sleep."

Toni shook her head.

"When was he found?" asked Agatha.

"Two hours ago."

"But Bill Wong phoned me not so long ago."

"He's off duty. Probably one of his colleagues at the station realized Miss Gilmour is part of the murder inquiry we're investigating and phoned him."

The doorbell rang. "Can't be your mother already," said Agatha.

"It'll be George," said Toni. "I got Maggie here to phone him."

Agatha felt slightly miffed that Toni had not thought to phone her.

George Pyson came into the room. "There's a bed and breakfast down the street. I've booked a double room for your mother and her friend. I know the owner. She's very kind. She says if I phone her when they are due to arrive, she'll get up to let them in."

"Do you want us to wait?" asked Agatha, feeling superfluous.

"No," said Toni weakly. "I think George will take care of everything. And my friend, Maggie, says she'll stay the night."

As they drove off, Agatha said, "You know, he must be interested in her. But he's too old."

"He's only in his early thirties and he's a good-looking fellow," said Charles. "Don't interfere."

"I've invested a lot of time and money in that girl," said Agatha. "Next thing, she'll be off, married to George and too pregnant to do any work."

"I never thought of you as being mercenary, Aggie."

"I'm a businesswoman, I'll have you know."

"Quite. But bug out."

TEN

†

PHIL, CHARLES and Agatha drove to Bourton-on-the-Water the following morning, after Agatha had telephoned Toni. Toni said her mother was actually sober and that delight had seemed to have taken some of the misery out of her brother's suicide.

"How did he kill himself?" asked Phil.

"Hanged. Drilled a hook into the kitchen ceiling and hanged himself from that, Toni says."

"That poor girl!"

"She had a miserable time with him," said Agatha. "I'll buy her a second-hand car when we're finished in Bourton." They drove into the car park and walked through to the village. "Would you look at that!" exclaimed Agatha. "Look at all the people and at this time of year. I think the tourists just never stop."

"Loads of Chinese," said Charles. "They're allowing them out on package tours to the Cotswolds."

Bourton-on-the-Water is a famous beauty spot with a glassy stream flowing through the centre: old bridges and old houses. The day was sunny and clear with a cold wind sending the last of the leaves scurrying along the street in front of them.

"It's round here."

"I wonder if this is really a good idea," said Agatha. "I always think psychiatrists are like fortune-tellers and psychics. People only go to them to indulge their vanity."

"People like you always think that," said Charles, turning to admire the back view of a pretty girl with long legs.

"What do you mean? People like me."

"People who need a psychiatrist themselves."

"That's snide."

"Think about it, Aggie. You're pining after an ex-husband who was a pain in the bum when you married him and you aren't even in love with him any more."

"I'll have you know, you miserable little, penny-pinching—"

"Children! Children!" admonished Phil. "We're here."

The house was small and grey; one of those old Cotswold houses which weather so well that it is hard to determine its age.

The door was opened by a tall rangy female in tight jeans, high boots and a peasant-type blouse. She had masses of frizzy blonde hair, a narrow face and pale-blue eyes.

"Wot you want?" she asked.

"Dr. Drayton."

"You 'ave the appointment?"

"Yes," said Phil. "Mr. Marshall."

"Wait."

"These Poles get everywhere these days," said Charles. "But what a looker!"

She returned. "Come in."

They followed her into a book-lined study where an elderly man sat in front of a log fire. He had thinning grey hair and very thick glasses. He was hunched forward in a leather armchair, wearing an old Harris tweed jacket with leather patches on the elbows.

"Sit down," he ordered. "Turn my chair round, Sasha, so I can see them."

Sasha did as she was told. "You may leave us," said Dr. Drayton.

"You want tea?"

"No, I don't think that will be necessary."

He might have asked, thought Agatha, looking around to see if there was an ashtray in the room and not finding any.

"Where did you find the girl?" asked Charles.

"An agency. Now, I believe you wish to consult me." He took a small tape recorder out of his pocket and switched it on.

Agatha began at the beginning. He interrupted her only occasionally to ask for descriptions of various people. Charles, who often put Agatha down as scatty, was amazed at the clear and concise report she gave.

When she had finished, Dr. Drayton said, "I wonder what her upbringing was like? Leave this with me and I will give you my conclusions. May I have your address?"

Agatha fished out a card and handed it to him.

"Thank you." He rang a small bell. Sasha appeared. "They are leaving," he said. "Show them out."

Sasha led the way to the front door. As Agatha and Phil walked down the short garden path, Charles nipped back before Sasha could close the door. They waited outside the garden gate. Agatha saw Charles giving Sasha his card.

It's all right for men, she thought sourly. He's in his middle forties and yet he can chat up a young girl like that. Now, if I chased after George Pyson, say, I'd be called a harpy.

Phil and Charles helped Agatha buy a small second-hand Ford. With Charles driving it and Agatha following after they had dropped Phil off at his cottage with stern instructions to rest, they went into Mircester and parked in the main square.

Toni had just returned from identifying the body. Her mother was red-eyed but composed. "I got you a car," said Agatha gruffly. "Here are the keys and the paperwork."

"Oh, thank you," said Toni. "You are so generous."

"I'm not really," said Agatha. "You can hand the car back to me if you ever leave. Where's George?"

Mrs. Gilmour said, "He's at the undertaker's to arrange the funeral. So kind."

I must warn her about George, thought Agatha. That was immediately followed by the sensible thought that she should really mind her own business. Toni and her mother needed all the help they could get. Agatha told Toni to take as much time as she needed. Then she asked, "What about your home, Mrs. Gilmour? Are you going back there?"

"No, I went over today and it's filthy. Fortunately I bought it when I was still working and council houses were cheap. Mr. Pyson is hiring two women to scrub the place out. I really don't know what we'd do without him."

"Right. Toni, I'll call you later in the day to see how you are."

Toni put her arms round Agatha and hugged her by way of farewell.

"How's about that?" asked Charles when they were outside. "Didn't know you had a maternal streak."

"Maternal be damned," snorted Agatha. "She's a good detective and I don't want to lose her."

"Looks to me as if you are going to lose her to George."

"Curse the man. Why couldn't he pick on someone older?"

"Like you?"

"Shut up! Let the moths out of your wallet for once and buy me lunch!"

Charles went off after lunch, leaving Agatha to return to the office on her own.

She found Alison waiting for her, an Alison pale-faced and fretful, who leaped up when Agatha entered, crying, "You must drop the investigation at once!"

"Why? Please sit down. You look awful. May we give you a cup of coffee?"

"No! No! Just drop it. I'll pay you anything you want. I've told the police I am taking you off the case."

"But why? Surely you'll want all this cleared up?"

Alison suddenly sank down on the sofa and burst into tears. Mrs. Freedman rushed forward with a box of tissues. Agatha paced up and down feeling helpless while motherly Mrs. Freedman sat beside Alison with an arm around her shoulders, saying, "There, now. Have a good cry, dear. It'll make you feel better."

Alison at last dried her eyes, gave a huge gulping sob, and said, "If you don't drop the case, Bert says he'll divorce me. He said things were bad enough before, but now you've discovered his mother was probably a murderer, they'll find it even harder to sell the house and estate."

Was that the real motive? wondered Agatha. Or had one of the family or all of them killed Phyllis and didn't want her to discover it?

"Don't you want to find out who killed Phyllis?" asked Agatha.

"Oh, I do," wailed Alison pitifully.

"Well, just go back and tell your husband that I am off the case. I'll try to find out something very quietly."

"Can't you just leave it alone? Bert says the police have all the resources you haven't, like forensics and all that."

"Forensics didn't do a very good job of finding that poisoned bottle of wine before it killed Fred Instick."

There was a long silence and then Alison said reluctantly, "All right. But it means you can't go near the manor."

"Then I'll have to rely on you to keep me informed," said Agatha. "Will you do that?"

"Very well."

When Alison left, Agatha went to the window and looked down. Bert was waiting on the other side of the road for her. She could see Alison talking rapidly and then Bert smiled, patted her back and gave her a kiss on the cheek.

"I'll find out who murdered that damn woman if it's the last thing I do," muttered Agatha.

But she was too busy in the following days, filling in for Phil, whom she had ordered to take more rest, and for Toni, who was not expected back at work until the following week.

Charles had disappeared again and so Agatha was glad of Roy Silver's company when that young man arrived for the weekend. She had forgotten what a good listener he was. On Saturday morning at the breakfast table, she told him all about the case from beginning to end and it was over an hour before she had finished.

He had listened carefully and then brightened when she told him about the visit to the retired psychiatrist. "Ooh! I would like to see him," said Roy. "He might find me a fascinating subject."

"And he might die of boredom."

"Claws in, Aggie."

"Don't call me Aggie!"

"So are we sleuthing this weekend?"

"Actually, I thought I'd make some plans for my Christmas dinner."

"Don't talk about Christmas," complained Roy. "I hate the whole business. Crowded shops. *Sound of Music* and *Miracle on 34th Street*, all running for the umpteenth time. People get so cross and worried and spend too much money and begin to hate their families. Some relatives always disgrace themselves by getting drunk."

"Roy, my Christmas is going to be one you'll never forget."

"I haven't quite forgotten the last one. Do you remember when you incinerated the Christmas pudding and lost your eyebrows?"

"I have learned from my mistakes. Alison has begged me to drop the case. I can't go near the manor."

"That Toni's an awfully pretty girl," said Roy. "She looked lovely on television. Wouldn't surprise me if some television people didn't snatch her up."

"Over my dead body," said Agatha.

"You've got all these suspects," said Roy. "In fact, it's beginning to look like the local phone directory. You've told me all about them and which one could have maybe murdered Phyllis, but you've left one out."

"Who's that?"

"George Pyson."

"He's only the factor," said Agatha. "He had only been working for her for four years. Why should he, of all people, want to kill her?"

"He runs the estate. He does the books. He could have been creaming off money and Phyllis could have found out and threatened to go to the police."

"So why was the gardener poisoned?"

"To cover up his first crime."

"No. The gardener was killed after he put his head round the drawing room door and told them he knew which one of them had done it. Not one of them had time to doctor that bottle of wine. Now I come to think of it, it may point to someone outside the family who didn't know that none of them liked the wine. Mind you, I don't really want to think of that because it would mean that all of them are at risk. It could have been one of those awful villagers. They're in a time warp. They believe in witchcraft and probably know an awful lot about poisonous plants. I'd like to go back to that village, but I doubt if any one of them would speak to us.

"Then there are those two sisters from the village who waited table. Maybe they did it. But why should they? With Phyllis gone and the family planning to sell, they'd risk losing their cheap rent. I wish I could take another look round Phyllis's bedroom."

"I'm sure the police turned it over thoroughly."

"Maybe not. I'll phone Alison and ask if there's any hope that the lot of them could all be out of the place sometime."

Agatha came back from phoning. "What luck? I phoned Alison on her mobile and she said they were all at Sir Henry's to get away from the press. She says Jill, the groom, will let us in. This letter's just arrived. The address on the back says it's from that psychiatrist."

"Do open it," begged Roy. "Maybe he'll have solved the murder for us."

Agatha opened the envelope and began to read. Roy waited impatiently. At last he said, "Well, come on. What does he say?"

"Load of bollocks."

"Tell me!"

"The sum total is that he believes Phyllis was a megalomaniac and poisoned herself in order to get revenge on the children she never really wanted to have."

"Isn't that possible?"

"When the poison began to take effect, she looked startled and worried."

"But she was found clutching that hemlock root, wasn't she?"

"She was wearing a dress with pockets. She might have popped the root in one of the pockets after making up the salads. She might have taken the root out of her pocket before she became totally paralysed to give us a clue. And why did she think she was going to be murdered, and by one of her family?"

"Aggie, the man's an expert. Why don't you just take his word for it?"

"I'm going to investigate further. Wait! I've got to phone Alison again."

Alison answered, saying in an urgent whisper, "You've got to stop phoning me. Wait. I'll go into the other room. Now, what is it?"

"The will divided everything equally amongst the four of you?"

"Yes."

"No mention of the technical college getting all the money?"

"No, but the lawyer said she had told him that she meant to visit him a week after her death to change her will. We all knew that."

"Talk to you later," said Agatha and rang off.

She turned to Roy, her eyes gleaming. "There you are. I'm slipping. I'd forgotten the one most important fact. Phyllis was going to change her will and if she hadn't been murdered, there's a good chance her family might have ended up with very little. Let's get going and hope there are no police up there."

After opening a few wrong doors, Agatha found Phyllis's room. The mattress and box spring had been removed, no doubt for forensic examination.

"Where do we start?" asked Roy.

"You poke around under the carpet and see if she could have hidden anything under the floorboards. I'll look through the bookshelves. Weird that she liked nothing but children's books."

Agatha began to take the books out of the shelves, shaking each one. "Why are you shaking the books?" asked Roy.

"Because there might be a draft of a will or a letter."

"You've been reading too many detective stories," said Roy. "I can't do anything with this carpet. It's nasty fitted haircord and nailed down."

"Well, just sit there."

Agatha at last straightened up. She gave a yelp of pain and clutched her hip.

"You should do something about that," said Roy.

"Shut up and let me think. I've been muddled up with all these suspects. I've a feeling the obvious is staring me in the face. Let me go back to that final, dreadful high tea. Fran threw a scene and threw her salad into the fireplace. Wait a minute! Before Charles and I went off to the pub, Charles wanted to look in on Phyllis, but Fran stopped him! Said she was just sleeping."

"It might have looked like that."

"The salads would be laid out in the kitchen before tea. Fran could have nipped in and grated hemlock into Phyllis's salad."

"How would she know which salad Phyllis would take?"

"Got to phone Alison."

"Oh," wailed Alison, "they're already getting suspicious. You're lucky I'm in my room. What is it now?"

"Did Phyllis have a favourite bowl for salad?"

"Yes, it was the blue one. Blue with yellow flowers."

"But I remember the others were blue with yellow flowers."

"The bowl Phyllis had was a deep blue. She got the set cheap because they were supposed to be matching in colour but one of the bowls had come out a darker blue than the others. So she knocked the price down. What's this about?"

"Talk to you later."

Agatha said to Roy, "She did have a favourite bowl."

"Yes, but Fran didn't have time to get back into the kitchen and look for a hemlock root," said Roy.

"She might have been in the habit of carrying bits of vegetables round in her pocket with her. Don't spoil my theory," snapped Agatha.

"But how on earth are you going to prove it?"

"I'll confront her. Help me to put these books back."

"Aggie, tell the police."

"Won't do. Fran knows there's no proof but she might drop her guard to me. I'll wait until they get back here and phone. I mean, I didn't see any press around."

"So if you can't get her now," pleaded Roy, "why don't we just spend the rest of the time having a lazy weekend?"

"After I see how Toni is getting on. I don't even know when the funeral is or was. I shouldn't have left everything to George Pyson. He's got designs on that young girl and he's too old."

"How old?"

"Early thirties."

"That's not old. Why interfere?"

The answer to that was, "Because I don't want to lose a very good detective," but Agatha said instead, "Hurry up with these books."

Toni was sitting in her flat with her friend, Maggie, when Agatha and Roy arrived. She thanked them for coming, struggling with her accent, which had reverted to the local speech, so that when speaking to Agatha it was her new "posh" one and to Maggie, the sing-song voice of Mircester.

"The funeral is tomorrow," said Toni. "George has been a saint. The house is all scrubbed and cleaned and my mother is putting it up for sale."

"And he's ever so handsome," breathed Maggie. She was a plump friendly girl with her black hair gelled into spikes, large chocolate-brown eyes, and a snub nose.

"You must regard him as a sort of father figure by now," Agatha said hopefully to Toni.

"No, just as a good friend."

"How are you coping?"

"Now I've got over the shock, all I feel is a sort of guilty relief. Is that terrible?"

"No, just human," said Agatha. "Where is your mother?"

"Showing people the house. Her friend is with her."

"I'll be back at the office on Tuesday afternoon. I want to start working again. Oh, Charles was very kind. He sent the most beautiful wreath."

"I forgot about flowers. I am so sorry," said Agatha, narrowing her small eyes and wondering whether it was Toni's looks which had prompted the normally mean Charles to open his wallet.

She felt old as she left with Roy, after promising to attend the funeral.

Agatha tried to phone Charles but got the usual rebuff from his butler, who seemed to delight in telling her that Charles was "not at home."

She did not want to subject Phil to any more danger, and Patrick, good and solid though he was, could be intimidating, as he looked like the policeman he used to be before he retired.

Agatha also felt she could no longer enlist Alison's help. After the funeral of Toni's brother, Agatha wrote to Fran saying that she was sure she had discovered the identity of the murderer and would Fran please telephone to make an appointment. Agatha suggested that Fran should not communicate this news to any of the others as it might unnecessarily upset them.

Feeling lonely and depressed by the funeral, which had taken place in a cold driving rain, Agatha decided that evening to call in Mrs. Bloxby. She felt she should really break the habit of just calling at the vicarage anytime she felt like it, just as if the vicar's wife did not have a life of her own. But if she phoned and the vicar answered, she knew he did not like her and would put her off.

Hoping the vicar would not answer the door, she made her way to the vicarage, comforting herself with the thought of the glorious Christmas dinner she meant to arrange, for the days were dark and dreary and the trouble with living in the countryside, thought Agatha, was that one was terribly aware of everything dying or settling down for a winter hibernation. In the city, with its lights and bustle, it was hard to notice the changing of the seasons.

To her relief, Mrs. Bloxby answered the door. "Am I interrupting anything?" asked Agatha.

"No, come in, Mrs. Raisin, and take off your wet coat. Alf has gone to a meeting over in Evesham. Would you like coffee or a sherry?"

"A sherry would be nice," said Agatha. Sherry was the only alcoholic drink served in the vicarage.

When they were settled, Mrs. Bloxby said, "You look worried."

"I've just thought of something," said Agatha. "I thought I had found out who murdered Phyllis Tamworthy and it seemed as clear as day. Now, I have doubts."

"Tell me about it."

So Agatha outlined all the facts that made her suspicious of Fran.

"I really don't like the idea of you asking her to call on you," said Mrs. Bloxby. "Wouldn't it be a good idea to tell the police?"

"Do you think they'd listen to my suppositions?"

"Maybe not. But I am sure Bill Wong would."

"He'd feel duty-bound to pass it on. Oh, well, it'll work or it won't."

"Don't drink anything when she's around!"

"No, I won't. I wish this case was all solved and I could get back to the more pedestrian work of the agency. Still, I've got Christmas to look forward to."

Mrs. Bloxby sighed. "It should be a happy festival, but no one these days looks forward to Christmas. So many people going bankrupt with those wretched shop credit cards. They hand them out to people who can't possibly afford the sums they run up." She clasped her hands nervously. "Mrs. Raisin, please do not build up too many expectations of Christmas."

"It'll be fun," said Agatha. "Just you wait and see."

Agatha returned to her cottage, deciding to go through her notes on the case. She always wrote up each of her cases and put them on disk in the fond hope that after she was dead, someone would write a book from them.

She found a missing capital *A* in the middle of a sentence

and decided to add it. But instead of pressing the cap key, by mistake she pressed the control button, capital *A,* and, for some mad reason, delete. She watched in horror as all her notes disappeared, leaving her with a blank page. In the panic induced in someone who suffered from techno fear, she scrolled through the computer in a desperate bid to find the missing file. The phone rang. Agatha switched off her computer and went to answer it. There was nothing but silence at the other end and then the sound of a receiver being replaced. I hope that wasn't mad Jimmy, thought Agatha uneasily. She phoned Roy and asked for help with her computer.

"It's all right," he said. "Just press the undo button at the top of the page. You didn't switch off the computer, did you?"

"Yes. Does that make a difference?"

"I don't think you're going to find that file. Sorry."

Agatha felt dismally that it was a bad omen.

ELEVEN

✝

AGATHA CHECKED the post the following days and had almost given up hearing from Fran, as she had expected her to write, when she received a phone call at the office.

It was Fran. She said, "I will see you privately to protect the family from your imaginings. I do not want to see you at the office. Where do you live? I will call on you this evening."

Agatha gave her the address and directions. They settled on the time of eight o'clock.

Plunging herself into the detective agency's cases, glad to see that Toni was once more on top form and Phil was looking his usual normal healthy self, Agatha tried to put the evening's appointment out of her head.

*   *   *

As eight o'clock approached, Agatha began to feel nervous. The phone rang, but it was Mrs. Bloxby. "I can't talk long," said Agatha. "I'm expecting Fran."

"Oh, Mrs. Raisin, do be careful."

"Don't tell anyone, mind? I have a feeling I am about to make a fool of myself."

"Do one thing for me. When you let her in, do not shut the front door entirely."

"Why?"

"You might want to escape quickly."

"I'll be all right."

"Please! Do it for me!"

"All right. I promise. Now, I'd better hang up. She'll be here any minute."

Mrs. Bloxby replaced the receiver and sat looking at it. Mrs. Raisin may never speak to me again, she thought. But this is something I feel I must do.

She picked up the receiver again, dialled Mircester police headquarters and asked to speak to Bill Wong.

By ten past eight, Agatha was beginning to wonder whether Fran had changed her mind. By half past eight, she was sure of it. At twenty to nine the doorbell rang. Fran stood on the step, unfurling a large gold umbrella.

"Come in," said Agatha. "Let me take your coat." Agatha left her front door very slightly ajar.

"I have only come to stop you from troubling the family further," said Fran.

Agatha took her coat and umbrella for her.

"Sit down for a moment and I'll tell you what is troubling me," said Agatha. In Agatha's cosy sitting room with a log fire blazing on the hearth, Fran sat on the edge of an armchair.

Looking at her, Agatha felt sure that such a weak-looking woman with her tightly curled hair and indeterminate features could not be capable of murder. But she surreptitiously switched on a tiny powerful tape recorder in her open hand-bag under the pretext of finding her cigarettes and decided to plunge in anyway.

"I've been thinking a lot about the murder of your mother," said Agatha.

"Did you bring me down here to tell me that?" asked Fran. "We all think about nothing else. I could do with a drink."

"What'll you have?"

"Gin and tonic."

Agatha, who longed for a drink herself, decided it would be safer not to have anything that Fran might be able to poison. She sliced lemon, dropped ice in a glass, put in a strong measure of gin and added tonic.

"There you are," said Agatha. "Now, where was I?"

Fran stared at her coldly over her glass. "You were about to explain the reason for my visit. You don't seem to have told the others about asking me to come here."

"I didn't tell anyone . . . yet," lied Agatha.

"So what's the reason?"

"Well," said Agatha, "it's just that I think you murdered your mother."

"You're mad! What is it, dear? The menopause? Or did you forget to take your pills today?"

"Why wouldn't you let Charles look at your mother after she had been taken up to her bedroom. You said she was asleep, but if you had taken a good look at her, you surely would have seen from her colouring that there was something seriously up with her. I think your mother had hemlock root in her pocket and with her last bit of strength she took it out and clutched it. I think she knew what had happened to her. You cold-bloodedly went away and waited for her to die."

"What absolute tosh. How on earth could anyone prove that?"

Agatha was struck with one of her rare intuitive flashes of insight. "The police have not really been looking closely at you, Fran. You're not really a countrywoman. You must have been out before the murder, searching for hemlock. Someone must have seen you. I bet the police did not search your house thoroughly. I bet you've got a little hemlock factory there, just in case you needed to get rid of anyone else. You'd have cleaned the place up after your mother's murder, but I bet once the coast was clear you went back to your old tricks. No, I haven't told anyone . . . yet. But as soon as you leave, I'm calling the police. You attacked me viciously when I said I was sure your mother's death was murder."

There was a brief glitter of panic in Fran's eyes.

She took a strong pull of her drink. Then she said, "If that's all the rubbish you've got to say, I'm leaving. But I would like to use your toilet first. The police can search until doomsday, but they won't find anything because I had nothing to do with it."

"Upstairs, on the left," said Agatha, feeling suddenly depressed. She must have imagined seeing that flash of panic.

Fran picked up her handbag and went up the stairs. Agatha waited a minute and then followed, her feet making no sound on the thick-carpeted stairs. The bathroom door did not have a lock, because Charles on one of his visits had broken it and Agatha had not yet had it repaired.

She pushed the bathroom door open a crack.

Fran had a syringe in her hand and was inserting the contents into a tube of toothpaste.

Agatha retreated to the sitting room, her heart beating hard. When Fran eventually returned, Agatha said, "And how were you planning to explain how you poisoned me?"

Fran turned a muddy colour. "I followed you upstairs. You put something in my toothpaste. I'm calling the police," said Agatha.

Fran flew at Agatha, clawing at her neck. She seemed to have amazing strength. Agatha kicked and struggled, tearing at the hands around her neck.

Then suddenly she was free, and Bill Wong, who had rushed in, forced Fran down onto the carpet and handcuffed her.

Fran lay still and silent. Bill phoned headquarters. He turned to Agatha. "You've put your life at risk again. What happened?"

Agatha explained. She finished by saying, "I don't know what you'll find in that toothpaste, but I bet it's lethal."

"It's a damn good thing Mrs. Bloxby phoned me." Agatha sank down on the sofa, her legs weak. Then she got up again. "I need to pee."

"Then go in the garden or a neighbour's house," said Bill. "You are not to go near your bathroom until a forensic team have taken everything out of it."

Agatha retreated to the garden. It was bucketing with rain and she felt sick and miserable. By the time she returned, Bill had lifted Fran up and thrust her into a chair.

"I had to do it," said Fran suddenly. "You must see that. After Father died, she was awful. She said she never wanted to have us anyway and started tightening the purse strings. It's her fault my daughter is a lesbian. Mother made our lives hell. All that money and she was not going to leave us anything. She had to be stopped."

"What about poor old Fred Instick?" asked Agatha.

"I poisoned one of those bottles in the hope that one of the village people would steal it. Then it would look as if someone outside of the family had it in for all of us. It was a justified crime. Fred was old, anyway."

"Did any of the others know you murdered your mother?" asked Agatha.

"Them? Rabbits, all of them. I suggested it and they all bleated, 'Don't even think about it.' Fools. She had made them suffer and yet they wouldn't do anything about it. Do you know why she kept having children? Father wanted to leave her. Every time he even thought about it, she'd contrive to get pregnant again. Wouldn't surprise me if at least one of us is a bastard."

They could hear the sound of approaching sirens. Fran lapsed into glassy-eyed silence.

Fran was formally charged and led away while Agatha braced herself for a long night of questioning.

Bill Wong was waylaid the following day by Detective Inspector Collins.

Agatha in a burst of rare generosity, because Bill had saved her, had credited him with helping her solve the mystery.

"Getting kudos all round," sneered Collins. "I heard that Raisin woman's tape. Talk about gifted amateurs. You had sod all to do with it. I'm getting a transfer to the Met."

"Don't invite me to your farewell party," said Bill over his shoulder as he walked off. He had tried to say that discovering the murderer had been all Agatha's work, but his bosses, ever mindful of the press, preferred to give him the credit. Also they felt that Agatha's mad guesswork would not be believed. They made it look as if Bill had arrived at the solution by methodical police work, particularly as a small bottle of distilled hemlock had been found in Fran's kitchen, marked "Cough Syrup."

Sir Charles Fraith learned about the solving of the murder on television and deeply regretted abandoning Agatha to go off chasing after Sasha, the psychiatrist's carer.

He decided that for once it might be a good idea to give Agatha a really good Christmas present. He phoned Roy Silver. After listening to Roy excitedly chattering on about the murder case and saying although Bill Wong got the credit, he was sure it was all Agatha's doing, Charles asked him if he had any idea what Agatha might like for Christmas.

After various suggestions such as a new watch, an evening gown, lingerie, Charles said, "Look, I'll take a trip up to London and maybe we can go round the shops together."

"I was supposed to be out at a photo shoot this afternoon," said Roy, "but it's been cancelled, so I was going to sneak the afternoon off."

"Where do you live?"

Roy gave Charles an address in Fulham.

"I'll set off now and pick you up."

But seeing things in the shops did not seem to make a choice easier. They decided to go to a bar in Jermyn Street and think it over.

"I'm intimidated by this famous dinner of hers," said Charles. "She wants it to be so perfect. Agatha's going to such a lot of expense—new oven, chef, caterers. She'll probably spend a fortune on decorations. She even thinks, I'm sure, that in the middle of global warming, it'll snow."

"That's it!" screeched Roy. "Brilliant!"

"What's brilliant?"

"We'll rent a snow machine, a real movie one. She plans to have tables from the dining room through to the sitting room. She'll be at the head of the table in the dining room. I'll nip out into the road just as the turkey is being brought in. I'll blow a whistle," said Roy, jiggling up and down in his seat with excitement. "You say, 'Look out of the window,' and, bam, I'll switch on the machine."

"You mean give her a white Christmas?"

"Exactly. We'll share the cost."

"She'll think we're awfully mean when we arrive without presents. Oh, damn, I've just remembered something. We needn't have bothered."

"Why?"

"Because I've got my invitation already and it says, 'No Presents.' What a waste of a day."

Roy stared at Charles, an unusually militant gleam in his eye. "It doesn't make any difference. She's our friend. I drop in at weekends, you use her cottage like a hotel, so it's payback time. Don't be so mean. She's going to have snow."

"Oh, very well," said Charles. "It can't go wrong, can it?"

"It'll be perfect."

Alison called on Agatha at her office that afternoon, just as Agatha was thinking of closing up for the day.

"They are all devastated at the news about Fran," she said. "Bert's beginning to come round. I pointed out to him that if that clever detective hadn't solved it, we'd all be under suspicion until the end of our days."

Agatha Raisin could not let that go past. "I let Bill take the credit," she said, "but it was me."

"How did you suddenly decide it was Fran?"

Agatha told her.

"And it's bound to come out in court that it was me," said Agatha, "because they need to produce that toothpaste as evidence, among other things."

"Haven't you heard? There isn't going to be a court case."

"Why?"

"Fran's dead."

"Did she poison herself?"

"No, she died of a massive heart attack."

"Snakes and bastards," muttered Agatha. She had been regretting letting Bill take all the credit and was looking forward to her day in court.

"I'll settle up my bill with you," said Alison.

"Mrs. Freedman's gone home. I'll get it sent to you tomorrow. Do you know, Phil Marshall got me to consult a police psychiatrist, a retired one, and the old boy told me Phyllis had committed suicide in such a way as to bring misery on her children. He's just sent me his bill. Eight hundred pounds. Cheeky old sod. He can sue me for it."

Two weeks later, Toni arrived outside her flat to find George Pyson waiting for her. "Thought you might like to come for a drink," he said.

Toni agreed nervously. He must be keen on me, she thought. He hasn't made a move, but if he does, then what do I do? I owe him so much.

But George was his usual amiable self. It turned out he wanted to know all about Fran.

Toni told him all that Agatha had described to her in the office after Fran was arrested.

"It's on the late news," said George. "Fran had a massive heart attack and died."

"Pity," said Toni. "I know Agatha was looking forward to her day in court."

"Why?"

"She let Bill Wong take all the credit, but it would have come out in the evidence in court that it was she who solved the whole thing."

"Strange woman," mused George. "Agatha, I mean. The way she crashes around, one wouldn't credit her with having one intuitive thought."

"She's very kind and generous. She's done a lot for me. You've done a lot for me. I don't know how I can ever thank you, George."

"You can thank me by forgetting about the whole thing. Managing things is my job and my weakness is managing other people's affairs."

A youth stopped at their table. He had gelled hair, a weak white face and was dressed in a denim jacket and torn jeans. "Hiya, Tone," he said.

"This is Pete Ericson," said Toni, introducing him to George. "We were at school together."

"How you doin', Tone," said Pete. "I hear you're a tec."

"Right, Pete," said Toni desperately, "and I'm on a case."

"Okay." Pete slouched off.

"Ashamed of me, Toni?" asked George.

"I never liked him and it was the easiest way to get rid of him," said Toni, feeling caught between two worlds. She wondered what Pete had been doing frequenting one of the smarter watering holes in Mircester.

They were not to be left alone. A hard-faced woman, elegantly dressed and expensively blonded, rushed up to their table and air-kissed George. "Darling, where have you been?" she screamed above the noise of the pub. "And who's this? Your niece?"

"This is Toni Gilmour, a friend of mine. Toni, Deborah Hasard." "Pleased to meet you," mumbled Toni.

"I've left my drink on the bar. I'll just get it and join you," said Deborah. The minute her back was turned, George hissed, "Let's go before she comes back."

They hurried to the door and out onto the street. "Old girlfriend of yours?" asked Toni.

"No, just a terrible bore. I'll get you home. How's the new car?"

"I love it. I take it for runs in the country, just like a dog."

"Perhaps you'll give me a run one day?"

"Sure. Here's my flat. Goodnight," said Toni firmly, "and thank you for the drink."

Later that evening, Toni looked down from her window and saw a group of her ex–school friends, chattering and laughing and obviously heading for the disco at the end of the street.

I've left them behind, thought Toni, and yet I feel I don't belong anywhere now. And what am I going to do about George?

Mrs. Bloxby called on Agatha that evening. "I really feel you should take a rest after all you've been through, Mrs. Raisin."

"No, I'm all right. I wonder if the Tamworthys will ever sell that estate. I think they were born unlucky and that they're doomed to be unlucky."

"Haven't you heard?"

"Heard what?"

"There was a little bit in the local paper. I brought it along." Mrs. Bloxby fished a newspaper out of her capacious handbag. "Here we are. Olde English Theme Parks are making an offer. They want to turn it into a theme park."

"What? Roundabouts and roller coasters and things like that?"

"No, they plan to turn it into an old English village with the locals dressed up in Georgian dress. The manor house will be demodernized and will serve old English teas. The great thing for the villagers is that they will live rent-free and be paid by the company to do things like spin wool and shoe horses."

"That jammy lot," howled Agatha. "They don't deserve it."

"Even Jimmy Tamworthy's shop is to be turned into an old-fashioned store."

"I wonder if those poxy villagers realize they have to be nice to the tourists."

"Maybe the tourists will think their sour faces are in period."

"Well, I never want to see any of them again. Anyway, I've got more important things on my mind."

"Such as?"

"Christmas."

TWELVE

†

AGATHA'S CHRISTMAS dinner was to be held on the eighteenth of December. In the days leading up to it, Toni had been taken off detective duties to prowl the shops with Agatha picking out Christmas decorations and decorating the tree.

Mindful of the fact that her cats loved real trees but shied away from fake ones, Agatha reluctantly settled on a fake Douglas fir.

Then there was a trip to a shop in London which made fake holly look exactly like the real thing.

The seating plan caused Agatha a lot of headaches. She would put James on her left and Charles on her right. Then she changed her mind. Charles might do something to irritate James. She would give Patrick the honour of sitting next to her. Would the women of the Carsely Ladies' Society mind being relegated to the far end of the table in the sitting room? Mrs. Bloxby must have pride of place in the dining room. Agatha hoped her husband, the vicar, would not be too sour. Then would Doris Simpson not expect a good place and, if she didn't get one, think it was because she was only a cleaner?

"Why don't you sort out the important people," suggested Toni, who was seated at the kitchen table with Agatha, helping her with the plans. "You could put Charles in the hall to host that table and Mr. and Mrs. Bloxby in the sitting room. Put Doris and her husband next to Charles. Is your ex going to turn up?"

"He sent me a letter. I got it last week. He said he would arrive on time. What about you, Toni? After all your work, I feel you should get to choose your place. Next to George?"

Toni hesitated. "Is there going to be anyone young there?"

"There's Miss Simms. But you want a man. I've got it. I've invited my ex-detective, Harry Beam. You'll like him and he's not that much older than you."

"Then you could put both of us in the hall with Charles and Doris and her husband and that would get rid of the least-favourite place. You're going to have trouble with the fires."

"Why? I want one log fire in the dining room and one in the sitting room."

"But there's not much space once the tables are set up and whoever is sitting with their backs to the fire is going to get scorched."

"Rats! I'm beginning to regret the whole thing."

"You could get those fake logs and have them burning when the guests arrive and by the time they have their welcome drinks, they'll have burned down."

"Fake this, fake that. It's not really the way I imagined it. I must have real mistletoe. Where should I hang it?"

Well away from me and George, thought Toni. "Why not above your chair at the head of the table?"

"Good idea. That'll stop me being kissed by a lot of odds and sods."

"What are you going to wear?" asked Toni.

"Something sexy."

Toni blinked. She thought women of Agatha's age should be past wanting to be sexy.

Toni said suddenly, "But that table across the hall means they will have to edge round it to leave their coats, and then if they are going to stand around with their drinks before dinner, there won't be any room."

"That's the curse of these small cottages," mourned Agatha. "I will not be defeated. I know: I'll have a marquee in the garden."

"Won't that be cold?"

"No, not these days. They put in heaters. I'll have clothes rails for the coats and a bar. They can't go through the kitchen. I'll have some sort of canvas tunnel up the side of the house which will lead straight into the marquee."

"This is all going to cost you a fortune," said Toni. "You could have hired a suite at the Hilton for less."

"It's going to be Christmas in my home, and that's that."

George Pyson was, at that moment, pacing up and down his mother's drawing room. "Out with it," she said at last.

"It's this girl." George ran his hands through his thick hair. "I'm keen on her but she's very young."

"How young?"

"Just newly eighteen."

"That *is* an age difference. Now if you were forty-five and she was thirty, it really wouldn't matter. But eighteen! What's her name?"

"Toni Gilmour."

"Antonia Gilmour. Is she one of the Guiting Power Gilmours?"

"No, she is one of the council estate in Mircester Gilmours and I'll bet she was actually christened Toni."

"Does she work?"

"As a detective for Agatha Raisin."

"That woman who gets herself into the newspapers? What's she like, this Raisin woman?"

"Tough, pushy, good hair, good legs, small eyes."

"American?"

"British."

Mrs. Pyson studied her son with a worried crease between her brows. She was a small, dainty woman with thick white hair and a neat figure.

"The point is this," she said. "If by any chance she is in love with you . . ."

"She's not. But she could be."

"The fact is that the person one loves at eighteen is hardly the person one is going to be in love with at twenty-four."

"I think she's old for her years."

"She won't be a virgin, not these days."

"I think she is, Mother. She has that untouched look."

"That untouched look could simply mean, 'Don't touch me, George.' "

"I should never have told you. I should have known you wouldn't approve."

"Is she by any chance related to that young man who hanged himself?"

"That was her brother."

"Oh, *George!*"

Bill Wong had romantic troubles as well. He had covered a burglary at a lingerie shop called Naughties in Mircester. A pretty sales assistant called Jade had taken his fancy. They had been out together a couple of times since the burglary.

Agatha had told Bill he could bring a girlfriend to her dinner and so he had invited Jade. He wondered uneasily what Agatha would make of her. She had dyed red hair of a violent colour and wore the minimum of clothes, even on cold days. She chewed bubble gum a lot. Her bubble gum was colour-coordinated to suit whatever she was wearing. If Jade was wearing purple, then she chewed purple bubble gum; if red, red bubble gum and so on. But she had large blue eyes and a perfect complexion and very long legs.

There'll be such a crowd, Agatha won't even notice her, Bill reassured himself. She'll be so taken up with James Lacey she won't, in fact, notice anyone else.

The next day, Agatha was returning to the office with Phil when she saw Alison on the other side of the street and hailed her. Alison crossed to meet her.

"I hear you've sold the place," said Agatha. "Congratulations."

"May I talk to you?"

"Of course. We'll go for a coffee. I won't be long, Phil."

Over coffee, Alison said, "It's weird. We've all dreamed so long of the freedom that money would bring us, but we're all still huddled together at the manor, waiting there until the builders arrive and we'll be forced to leave. Jimmy sits surrounded by travel brochures but he never books anything. Bert drinks and smokes a lot and plays games on his computer. He barely talks to me."

Alison's eyes were red-rimmed with recent crying.

"Any of you thought of therapy?"

"No, I hate that idea."

"Why don't you go away yourself? You've got your own money. Go off, say, for a week, somewhere sunny."

"I couldn't leave Bert."

"If he's drinking and playing computer games all day long, then he's left you."

"Maybe I'll try that."

They'll never get rid of the dreadful Phyllis, thought Agatha, as she made her way up to her office. She put them all in an emotional prison and they don't even want to get out.

Three days before Agatha's Christmas dinner, Mrs. Pyson heard the sound of a vehicle coming up the drive of her house. A young girl came into view driving a rental van.

Mrs. Pyson went out to meet her.

The girl jumped down and held out her hand. "I'm Toni Gilmour. I'm a friend of your son."

"And what can I do for you, Miss Gilmour?"

"George kindly gave me some pieces of furniture from your home. I don't need them now. I'm buying my own stuff."

"Leave them in the van and come inside. I'll phone the village and get a couple of young men to put the stuff back in the attic."

She certainly looks presentable enough, thought Mrs. Pyson. Toni had let her long hair grow and it was now swept back in a French pleat. She was wearing corduroy trousers, a leather jacket, half-boots and a cashmere sweater she had found in a thrift shop.

"Would you like some tea?" asked Mrs. Pyson after she had telephoned for help to move the furniture.

Toni looked trapped but she murmured, "Yes, thank you. Can I help you?"

"No, I have help." Mrs. Pyson rang a bell on the table beside her. A tall girl with Slavic cheekbones came into the room.

"Tea," said Mrs. Pyson. "And some of those biscuits, Svetlana, that I bought the other day at the church sale."

When Svetlana had left, Mrs. Pyson said, "I never really approved of the European Union, but I must say, with the influx of immigrants from Eastern Europe one can get all the help one needs these days. I believe you are a detective. How did you meet my son?"

As Toni talked, Mrs. Pyson studied her. Clear voice. Practically no accent at all. Such a pity she's so young.

The tea arrived. "What do you plan to do with your life?" asked Mrs. Pyson. "I am sure all young girls want to get married."

"I shall never marry," said Toni.

"Nonsense. Why?"

"Careers last. Men don't."

"So young and so cynical! So what do you plan to do?"

"It's difficult," said Toni. "Mrs. Raisin gave me a break. She got me a flat, a car and she is paying me a good wage. And yet . . ."

"And yet?"

"I feel awfully grateful to her and to George."

"And it is weighing you down?"

Toni looked at her gratefully. "You see, I've been thinking how nice it would be to be a real detective."

"Aren't you one already?"

"Yes, but I mean join the police force. It's awful knocking on doors and asking questions when I don't really have any authority."

"Is that why you are returning the furniture? Because you do not want to be grateful to my son?"

Toni coloured up. "Something like that."

"Well, you must do what you want. I see two young men have arrived. We'd better go out and supervise the unloading."

When Toni had left, Mrs. Pyson sat down again, feeling sad. "Poor George," she said. "Why couldn't he pick on someone his own age?"

Agatha left Patrick, Phil, Toni and Mrs. Freedman to run the agency just before the day of her Christmas dinner. She was already feeling exhausted. So many trips to get just the right stuff. Up to London again to find Christmas crackers that had interesting things inside of them instead of the usual paper hats and plastic toys.

Then, what to wear? Black was flattering to her middle-aged figure but surely too funereal. Tiny little skirts were in fashion and her legs were good. But women like herself dressed in too youthful a fashion ended up looking older. She settled at last on a black velvet skirt with slits up both sides and a cherry-red silk blouse with a plunging neckline. The skirt demanded high heels and her hip was getting worse.

But this one night must be the best and everything must be sacrificed for it. She bought a pair of high-heeled sandals in black patent leather.

Miss Simms, Carsely's unmarried mother, was in a quandary. Her latest "gentleman friend" had just told her he was going back to his wife. Miss Simms had told Agatha she was bringing him along. She desperately needed an escort. She chewed nervously at her false nails, remembered what they had cost and poured herself a stiff vodka and Red Bull instead.

There was a knock at the door. Miss Simms opened it. One of those young men who sell dusters and other household stuff round the doors started his spiel, "Here is my card. I am unemployed."

Miss Simms didn't listen. Instead she eyed him up and down. He was well built with thick brown hair and a square pleasant face. She interrupted him. "Come in for a drink. I've got a suggestion to make."

Mrs. Bloxby and her husband did not often row. But on the eve of Agatha's dinner party they found themselves shouting at each other.

"I've told you and told you," yelled the vicar, "that I will not go to the Raisin female's party and that's that. I have promised to lead the carol service at Ancombe."

"You knew all about this party," said Mrs. Bloxby. "You only took on this carol service to get out of it."

"I did not."

"I talked to the vicar's wife over in Ancombe and she told me you were quite pressing about wanting to help. Her husband is taking the carol service and yet you offered to help when no help was needed."

The vicar looked mulish.

"Let's put it this way. I'm not going."

"Let's put it this way," shouted Mrs. Bloxby. "I am tired, sick and tired of your selfishness. I wear myself out with parish visits which you should be making. You control the purse strings. When did I last have a new dress? When did we last have a holiday?" And with that, the vicar's wife burst into tears.

"Oh, I am so sorry." The vicar's voice trembled. "I never thought . . ."

He handed her a clean handkerchief and then wrapped his arms around her. "Don't cry. We shall go to Agatha's and you can have a splendid new dress. And . . . and after all the Christmas services are over, why don't we take a short holiday, somewhere sunny?"

Mrs. Bloxby detached herself from him and dried her eyes. "Do you promise?"

"With all my heart. I do love you. You must know that."

She gave him a weak smile.

"Now, what about a cup of tea?"

A frosty gleam appeared in his wife's eyes.

"I'll get it," said the vicar hurriedly. "I'll get it!"

*   *   *

Agatha's nerves were on edge. The great day had arrived, but the weather was unseasonably warm and there was no sign of James. The men were erecting the marquee in a depressing drizzle.

Toni, Doris Simpson and Mrs. Bloxby arrived to help. The rooms were already decorated, but Agatha had decided to put the tree in the marquee so they would all need to wait until the men were finished.

Toni, sitting at the kitchen table, wrote out place cards on stiff cardboard. She also wrote on the cards that a bus had been hired to take the Mircester guests home at midnight and that the same bus would bring them back the next day to pick up their cars. Doris had previously taken Agatha's cats to her home because Hodge and Boswell were spending too much of their cunning time trying to get at the huge turkey lying in all its glory on the kitchen counter.

Crates of champagne and wine had arrived. The caterers were supplying extra tables, tablecloths, plates and glasses.

At last the men came in to say the marquee was ready, just as Roy arrived from London in an all-white suit with a sprig of holly in his lapel.

They carried the large tree, propped outside the front door, along the canvas tunnel at the side of the house and into the marquee. Then they returned to the house to go up to the spare room where the tree decorations were stored and carry them to the marquee as well. Roy had brought an overall with him to cover his precious suit. He whistled happily as he started by pinning a silver star on the top of the tree. "I see you've got coloured lights," he shouted down. "Too naff. White lights are the new black."

"Coloured lights," insisted Agatha grimly. "Oh, do get a move on!"

By five o'clock, Agatha got Roy to open a bottle of champagne. The chef was already busy in the kitchen, roasting the turkey and shouting at his assistants.

"Do you think a dinner will ever come out of this chaos?" moaned Agatha.

"It'll be all right on the night," said Roy.

"This is the night, you cloth head."

"No need to be a bitch, Aggie, just because there's no sign of your ex."

"If James doesn't come, it's all the same to me," protested Agatha, suddenly feeling sick at the thought he might not arrive and the waste of all this expense.

The guests were due to arrive at seven o'clock for drinks in the marquee, followed by dinner at eight.

Doris Simpson and Mrs. Bloxby went home to change and Agatha and Toni retreated upstairs to do the same.

Roy shouted after them that he was going to write a large sign saying "Agatha's Party" and put it over the entrance to the tunnel. "Otherwise," he called up the stairs, "they'll be ringing the doorbell and you'll need to go out in the rain to show them where to go." Roy thought happily of the snow machine resting in the small van he had hired. He couldn't wait to see Agatha's face.

Half an hour later, Roy called again that the barman had arrived along with the first guests, but where was Agatha?

At quarter past seven, Agatha made an appearance in the marquee and quickly scanned the guests. No James. Toni was wearing a simple black sheath with a broad scarlet belt round her slim waist. Her hair was brushed down on her shoulders. George Pyson was talking to her. Mrs. Bloxby was resplendent in a pretty smoky-blue chiffon dress, smiling up at her husband, her face radiant. Now that's real love, thought Agatha wistfully.

Soon, with the exception of James, everyone had arrived. Agatha longed to postpone the dinner for a little longer but felt sure the temperamental chef in the kitchen would murder her.

Harry Beam was talking to Bill Wong's girlfriend, a tarty creature with thick make-up and a see-through blouse. Toni had started to talk animatedly to Bill Wong and ignore George, who was hovering behind her. Miss Simms had arrived accompanied by some knuckle dragger, as Agatha inwardly damned him.

Agatha encountered a glare from the chef, who had marched into the marquee and reluctantly called out, "Dinner is served."

The guests oohed and aahed at the decorations as they searched for their places. Agatha noticed that Bill Wong was not sitting next to his girlfriend but next to Toni, and Harry Beam was now seated next to Bill's girlfriend. Agatha wondered if Toni had changed the place cards.

Everyone pulled crackers, the caterers poured wine and the first course of chestnut soup was served. Agatha was miserably aware of the empty place beside her. Then, just as the second course, smoked salmon, was appearing on the table, there was a ring at the doorbell. Agatha jumped to her feet, but Charles, seated in the hall, shouted he'd get it.

James Lacey walked in. "Your place is here!" called Agatha, her face radiant.

He walked up to her and bent down to kiss her on the cheek. Agatha drew back and pointed to the large bunch of mistletoe above her head. He smiled and wrapped his arms around her, bent his head, and kissed her passionately on the mouth.

And Agatha felt nothing.

When he drew back, he looked down at her with a puzzled frown.

"Oh, do sit down, James," said Agatha, all false jollity. "You've missed the first course but you're in good time for the salmon and the turkey."

Oh dear, thought Mrs. Bloxby, as Agatha bent her head over her plate and studied the smoked salmon as if it was the most interesting thing she had ever seen.

Jade, Bill Wong's girlfriend, was flirting outrageously with Harry Beam.

Toni and Bill Wong had their heads together in animated discussion. Miss Simms's boyfriend was poking at his smoked salmon, shouting, "What's this muck?"

George Pyson felt very lonely. He had nourished such hopes for this evening.

Toni, once she had started talking to Bill, had barely looked at George.

The plates were cleared away. The chef appeared in the doorway with the magnificent roasted turkey on a trolley.

"Wait!" shouted Charles. He took out a whistle and blew a loud blast.

"What on earth . . . ?" began Agatha.

"Go to the window," called Charles, "and look out. It's a surprise."

Agatha went to the dining room window and looked out and then stared in amazement.

"It's snowing!" she cried. "It's really snowing."

There was an excited scraping back of chairs. Those in the sitting room opened their window; those in the hall opened the door. Agatha swung open the casement window, wide.

Roy crouched in the darkness with the snow machine and, slightly tipsy because he had been fortifying himself with brandy, was delighted with the reaction. "See if I can get some more," he muttered. He fiddled with the dials. But he accidentally turned the dial to "blizzard."

One minute, Agatha Raisin was framed by the window, looking out at gently falling snow. The next moment, she had turned into a snowman. She turned slowly, her beady eyes glaring out from her white snow-covered face.

Screams and yells and the crash of broken glass came as the guests reeled backwards before the arctic blast; curses as windows and door were wrenched shut.

But not before Charles had run out through the blizzard, thrust Roy aside, and switched the machine off.

There was a sudden silence.

"You may as well all go home," Agatha said wearily. Wet, papery snowflakes melted in her hair and dribbled down her face like tears.

Then Miss Simms began to laugh. It was an infectious throaty laugh.

Everyone began to join in. James shouted above the laughter, "This is a Christmas to remember. Here's to Agatha!"

Agatha jolted herself out of her misery. She turned to the chef. "We don't want the turkey to get cold. Thank goodness the snow missed it. Get your girls in here to clear up the broken glass. Who the hell thought up this idea?"

"Me and Roy," said Charles. "We did so want to give you a white Christmas."

"I'll kill you later. Chef, start carving. Girls, we need lots of paper towels so everyone can dry themselves off."

Agatha ran upstairs to change her clothes and repair her make-up. When she returned, everyone was sitting over large plates full of turkey and all the trimmings.

"Agatha," said James, "you never fail to surprise. Just listen to everybody. Your party's a big success."

"I don't know why they don't want to lynch me," said Agatha. "Mrs. Bloxby's got on a beautiful new dress. I hope it isn't ruined."

"Eat your turkey and stop worrying. It's the best turkey ever."

Agatha looked up at his handsome face and at his blue eyes and tried to reanimate some of that old passion, but nothing came.

Roy had reappeared and was chattering to everyone between mouthfuls of turkey and avoiding looking down the table in Agatha's direction.

Patrick said, "Everyone's drinking rather a lot. How are they all going to get home?"

"I've hired a bus to come at midnight to take the Mircester lot home. At ten the following morning, it will pick them up in the square and bring them back to Carsely to pick up their cars. Toni left a note about that with their place cards."

After the turkey, a huge plum pudding in all its flaming glory was brought in, along with plates of mince pies and tubs of brandy butter and dishes of whipped cream.

Agatha talked to Patrick about the Tamworthy case and then realized it looked as if she was pointedly ignoring James and turned back to him. He said he had been out of touch with the news on his travels, so Agatha told him about the murders.

"Toni?" he asked when she had finished. "Is she here?"

"She's the blonde girl talking to Bill Wong."

"Very young and beautiful," commented James. "I hope Bill doesn't get his heart broken."

Agatha felt a stab of jealousy. Bill Wong was her friend, her very first friend. Oh, well, if he took Toni to meet his mother and father, that would be the end of that. The dinner finished with three cheers for Agatha and then they all moved back to the marquee, where liqueurs and mulled wine were being served.

It was hard to feel dismal, thought Agatha, when everyone, even the knuckle dragger, kept telling her what a marvellous evening it had been. Even the vicar, a little bit tipsy, confided in her that he hadn't wanted to come but it had all been so wonderful, he was glad he hadn't missed it.

James was constantly at Agatha's side. Charles noticed that although Agatha looked happy, she didn't have that look of anguished exhilaration she used to have whenever James was near.

Agatha said to Mrs. Bloxby, "Your gorgeous gown doesn't seem to have suffered."

"Guess what, Mrs. Raisin. Alf and I are going on holiday at the New Year. It's only a package deal to Tunisia, but just think! Sunshine and no complaining parishioners."

At last the bus arrived to take the Mircester crowd home. Agatha stood outside her cottage to wave them off. She noticed that Bill was sitting next to Toni and Harry Beam next to Jade while George had a seat on his own.

As the bus rolled away, George reflected that he had a chance of a job on an estate in Sussex. He had dreamed of taking Toni with him as his wife. But Toni seemed to have forgotten his very existence.

James tried to kiss Agatha goodnight and looked surprised when she quickly turned her cheek. Charles and Roy were staying the night.

"Now, Roy," said Agatha when James had gone. "How could you do that to me?"

"We both did it," said Charles. "If Roy hadn't hit the wrong button, it would have been a great success. But look at it this way. No one is ever going to forget Agatha Raisin's Christmas dinner!"

EPILOGUE

✝

THE MIRCESTER guests arrived the following morning and were served with coffee and Alka-Seltzer in the marquee. Agatha felt sorry for George. Toni was obviously trying to be polite to him but kept breaking away and returning to Bill Wong.

James arrived to say he was leaving for his sister's and would stay there over Christmas. He longed to ask Agatha to go with him. After avoiding her for so long, he found he could not bear her new indifference—but he knew his sister did not approve of Agatha.

He said a reluctant goodbye, not even trying to kiss her this time, afraid of a rebuff.

Bill came up to Agatha, his eyes shining. "Toni says she'll come to my home for Christmas dinner." And that will be that, thought Agatha. His parents will soon see Toni off.

After the bus had left, Agatha, Roy and Charles went into the cottage. Agatha stared in dismay at the mess. The caterers had taken away the spare tables and cloths, but fake snow still lay on the floor and on the decorations.

"I thought the stuff was supposed to be biodegradable," said Charles.

"But it is," said Roy. "We can vacuum the stuff off the floor. Where's the sitting room furniture, Agatha?"

"It's in storage, and thankfully so are the pictures, ornaments and fiddly bits. I'll give you the vacuum, Roy. What about the stuff all over the walls and decorations?"

"That washes off." Both Charles and Roy were desperately thinking of ways to get out of cleaning the place, but Agatha stood over them while they groaned and worked.

The minute the place was comparatively clean, both said they must rush off.

Agatha said goodbye and then collected her cats from Doris.

After all the hustle and bustle of the previous days, the cottage felt empty and lonely. "Six days to Christmas," said Agatha gloomily to her cats, "and nowhere to go."

On Christmas day, Agatha went out for a long lonely walk. She decided to take the decorations down when she returned without waiting for the Twelfth Night. So depressing to sit on one's own and stare at all the baubles. She wondered with a grim smile how Toni was surviving Christmas dinner with Bill's parents.

"This is Toni," said Bill proudly, as his mother opened the door. Mrs. Wong peered at Toni through thick glasses and wiped her red hands on her apron. "I didn't know we were having extra company," she said. "Oh, well, take her into the lounge."

Mr. Wong was sitting reading a newspaper. He lowered it reluctantly when Bill introduced Toni. Bill served sweet sherry in tiny glasses. Mr. Wong had the same almond-shaped eyes as Bill but the rest of him was depressed British, from his droopy moustache to his ratty cardigan and carpet slippers. He raised his newspaper again. Toni saw nothing odd in his silence.

"How clever of your mum," she said to Bill, "to keep the plastic covers on her three-piece suite. She'll never have to worry about getting it dirty."

"My mother's very house-proud," said Bill.

Then there was a long silence. Mr. Wong rattled his newspaper nervously. He was used to Bill's girlfriends chattering to fill up the silence. Toni didn't bother.

"Dinner," shouted Mrs. Wong.

Mrs. Wong was usually a dreadful cook. Toni was in luck. The soup was tomato out of a can. Toni loved tomato soup. This was followed by a turkey already roasted at the local supermarket. Toni ate with relish. The Wongs did not seem odd to her. If one comes from a dysfunctional family, then the unacceptable becomes acceptable.

After the dinner was over, Toni insisted on following Mrs. Wong into the kitchen. Although there was a large dishwasher, every plate had to be scrubbed clean before being put into the machine. Toni talked happily about the murder case.

When it was time to leave, she flung her arms around the startled Mrs. Wong, hugged her and said, "Thank you for a wonderful meal."

And Mrs. Wong said for the first time in her life, "Call again."

Agatha was just taking down branches of fake holly when her phone rang. She rushed to answer it in the hope that someone actually wanted her company.

It was Alison, her voice breaking with hysteria. "They killed him! The villagers have killed him."

"Calm down. Take a deep breath and speak slowly," ordered Agatha. "Who's been killed?"

"Jimmy. They hanged him in that room above his shop, put a black candle under him and all sorts of cabalistic drawing painted in red on the walls."

"Have you called the police?"

"Yes."

"I'll be right there."

Alison met her in the hall. "They're all in the drawing room, except Sadie. She's being interviewed by the police in the dining room. I can't take any more of this, Agatha."

Agatha went into the dining room. Sir Henry Field was staring out of the window. Bert was slumped in a chair, staring sightlessly ahead.

Sadie came in. "Your turn next, Alison."

Alison sighed and got to her feet.

"It's awful," said Sadie. "Those villagers and their witchcraft." She stared at Agatha. "What are you doing here?"

"Alison sent for me."

"She had no right to do that. You are nothing but a muck-raker. Get out!"

"When Alison tells me to."

"This is not Alison's house and I am telling you to go. God, I need a cigarette."

Sadie bent down and unclasped her handbag. Agatha stiffened. She caught a glimpse of an envelope in Sadie's bag, and under one of Sadie's nails was what looked like red paint.

"Who found the body?" asked Agatha.

"Sadie did," replied Bert.

"And you are sure it was not suicide?"

"How could it be?" demanded Sadie. "Poor Jimmy would hardly hang himself and then light a candle and paint the walls."

"He could have done all that beforehand," said Agatha.

"Don't be so silly. I do wish you would go away."

"Right," said Agatha. She got to her feet and walked out.

But she went straight to the dining room. A policeman on guard outside tried to bar her way but Agatha pushed past him. Wilkes and Bill were interviewing Alison. They looked at Agatha in surprise, who was struggling to get free of the policeman's grasp.

"It's urgent," said Agatha. "I must speak to you now."

"All right. But it had better be good. We'll call you back when we're ready, Mrs. Tamworthy," Wilkes said.

Agatha said to Alison, "Don't tell them I'm still here."

"Now," said Wilkes severely, "explain yourself."

"There is an envelope in Sadie's handbag," said Agatha. "So?"

"And there is what looks like red paint under one of her nails."

225

Wilkes studied her for a long moment. A policewoman was sitting in a corner where she had been making notes. "PC Gold," said Wilkes. "Bring Lady Field back in here and make sure she brings her handbag with her."

Soon they could hear Sadie's voice raised in anger as she was escorted across the hall. "This is police harassment. I shall speak to my member of parliament."

The door of the dining room opened. Sadie's face turned red with anger when she saw Agatha. "I want that woman out of my house," she yelled.

"Sit down, Lady Field," ordered Wilkes. "Put your handbag on the table. Now spread out your hands."

Sadie spread out shaking hands. "What is that red under your fingernail?" asked Wilkes.

"Oh, that. Nail varnish. Now, if you're finished . . ." Then she let out a squawk of alarm as Wilkes opened her handbag and stared in. Under Sadie's terrified gaze, he put on a pair of latex gloves and extracted a letter from the bag. "This says quite clearly on the front 'To Whom It May Concern.' May I ask you what is in it?"

"No, you may not," panted Sadie. "It . . . it's my will. Have you a search warrant?"

"No, not yet. But either you let me open this or I will take you to headquarters and lock you in a cell until I get it. Take your pick."

Sadie seemed to shrivel. "I couldn't bear it," she whispered. "Poor Jimmy."

"Is that a yes?"

Sadie nodded miserably.

Wilkes opened the letter. He read it and then looked sternly at Sadie. "This is clearly from your brother, Jimmy Tamworthy. He states he cannot go on living. So I believe it was you who placed the black candle under him and it was you who painted the walls."

Between sobs, Sadie told them she had always hated the villagers. She didn't want the world to know that Jimmy had committed suicide.

"Take her down to headquarters," said Wilkes, "and inform her husband."

Sadie was led off by Bill and PC Gold.

Wilkes said to Agatha, "You have really surprised me this time, Mrs. Raisin."

"Why?"

"Finding out that Fran was the murderer has been a bit of a joke around the station. You had no forensic evidence, you had no proof at all, and yet you blunder on happily, getting the woman to call on you, and accusing her of murder. If she had not been slightly deranged, she could have let you witter on and got away with it.

"But I must admit, you do have a sharp eye—and the luck of the devil. I'd better get after them and wind this up."

"What will happen to her?" asked Agatha.

"Nothing, I would guess. She'll get a top psychiatrist to say her mind had been turned with all the tragedies. She can afford the best QC. Oh, yes, she'll get off with a slap on the wrist."

When he had gone, Agatha joined Bert and Alison. "When are you leaving this damned place?" she asked.

"We don't need to move until the end of January," said Bert.

"Move now!" howled Agatha. "Get out. Get away."

"I was staying out of respect for Mother's memory," said Bert.

"You're stark, staring bonkers. Read my lips. Your mother was a murderess. She reared a mentally sick family. So Fran killed her and poor Jimmy was too weak and pathetic to let himself live."

"Just go," said Bert in a tired voice.

Alison followed Agatha out. "I've had enough," she said. "If I stay with Bert I'll turn out as mad as this family."

"Where will you go?"

"Anywhere. Out of the country would be a good idea. I've been corresponding with an old friend who lives in Spain. I'll take a holiday and go and stay with her."

"What a horrible woman Phyllis Tamworthy was," said Agatha. "She murdered Jimmy just as if she'd strung him up herself."

Agatha hailed the new year with relief. Back to work. Back to taking on unsavoury court cases to make up for all the expense of Christmas.

She could hardly wait to ask how Toni had got on with Bill's parents. "They're so sweet," said Toni. "They invited me back for New Year."

"Are you and Bill an item?" asked Agatha.

Toni blushed. "We are, rather."

Agatha's heart sank. She could imagine what would happen if Toni married Bill. She would lose a good detective and one best friend all in one go. She had been hurt that Bill had not called to wish her a Happy New Year. Now she knew the reason.

And how had Toni managed to charm Bill's parents when all she had ever had from them was rudeness?

Charles hadn't phoned, but then he had never bothered in the past. Nor had Roy. Agatha had expected that the suicide of Jimmy might have prompted either of them to call her. Mrs. Bloxby was away on holiday.

Agatha sighed. Work was the answer. Work had always been the answer.

A cold wet winter dragged on into a cold wet spring. And then, at the end of April, the sun shone again, drying the countryside and bringing colour to the gardens and hedgerows.

Roy descended on Agatha one weekend. He had not even bothered to phone and she was tempted to tell him she was busy, but she was too glad of his company to send him away.

"Why the long silence?" asked Agatha. "I thought you might have phoned up about Jimmy, or to wish me a Happy New Year."

"I was very busy," said Roy huffily. "And the phone works both ways, you know. Anyway, it's gorgeous weather. What about a trip in the countryside?"

"Funnily enough I was thinking of taking a run over to Lower Tapor."

"Why on earth? Haven't you had enough of that place?"

"I just wanted to see what this theme park looks like. Evidently, it's up and running."

"Okay. Let's hope nobody murders anyone. How did Toni get on at that court case? You know, the woman who pushed the publican over the cliff."

"Very well. Elsie got life. Oh, there's another thing. Bill and Toni are dating."

"That's great."

"Won't last," said Agatha hopefully. "I keep having a feel-ing Toni's trying to work up courage to tell me something."

"Probably that she's going to get married or that she's pregnant."

"Don't even think about it! Let's go."

They had to pay an entrance fee and park in a field, still muddy after all the rain, and walk a good distance into the village. "Walk, walk, walk," groaned Roy. "Do you remember the first time we came here?"

They walked into the village and down into the village green. A maypole had been erected and sulky-looking chil-dren were dancing around it. In front of the pub, Morris Men were dancing lethargically. The locals were wandering about dressed in cod eighteenth-century clothes. They looked as sulky as ever. Doris Crampton was sitting outside her cottage staring mulishly at a spinning wheel.

"The only thing eighteenth-century about this place is the atmosphere," grumbled Roy. "Oh, look at that."

At a corner of the green stood a horse and carriage with a notice pinned on one carriage door: "Five pound carriage ride to the manor."

"Daylight robbery," said Agatha. "Let's go anyway."

The fee turned out to be five pounds each, but Agatha was too interested to see what had happened to the manor to protest.

They jolted along and then through the farm gates they had encountered on their first visit. In one field, a man was plough-ing with horses.

"You know, I bet all the villagers hate this," said Agatha,

"but if they don't start smiling and doing their jobs, this place will soon close down."

They were set down outside the manor. The stables now bore a large sign, AUTHENTIC OLDE ENGLISH TEAS.

A white sign outside the entrance door bore the legend NEXT TOUR: FIVE MINUTES.

"This gets worse and worse," said Roy. "There can't be anything worth seeing."

"Let's go anyway. People are already lining up."

The line soon began to shuffle forward. Inside the door, Doris's sister, Mavis, was sitting behind a desk with a roll of tickets. Her stout figure was encased in a black gown and she had a mob cap on her head. "Two pounds each," she said.

"We've already paid a fortune for the bleeding carriage," snarled Agatha.

"Oh, it's you," said Mavis. "Doesn't matter. That'll be four pounds altogether."

Agatha paid up and walked into the hall, which was lit by candlelight. And standing in the hall was their guide with a white powdered wig on and a panniered gown. It was Alison.

"What are you doing here?" exclaimed Agatha.

"Shhh!" admonished Alison. "I've got a break after this tour. I'll take you for tea and tell you about it."

The tour began. Unlike the villagers, Alison seemed to be throwing herself into her role. "We will start with the dining room," she said, "which is haunted by the ghost of Mrs. Tamworthy, the late owner, who was foully murdered—with hemlock!"

The dining room was now panelled and a small Victorian fireplace had been ripped out to be replaced by a large Georgian one where a log fire blazed.

Alison described the murder in gruesome detail. Agatha reflected that Alison was very good at her job. She led her tour from room to room. The kitchen had been remodelled into a period one and the visitors were interested in all the old kitchen equipment. A grumpy man was turning a leg of lamb over a spit.

Upstairs, the rooms had been re-enlarged to their original size and boasted four-poster beds.

All the rooms were lit by tall candles. Alison described what life would have been like for guests and servants in the eighteenth century. She's actually worth the entrance fee, thought Agatha.

When the tour was over, Alison led them over to the tea room. "It's like this," she said when they were seated. "Just after the New Year, when I got back from visiting my friend in Spain, I found Bert had left me. Just like that. Cleared off to Marbella. Bought a flat once the will came through. His excuse was that he didn't want anything, including me, to remind him of his mother. Can you beat it?"

"But you were going to tell him *you* had left *him*," said Agatha.

"I felt too sorry for him. I just said I was taking a holiday."

"So why did you take this job?" asked Agatha.

"The manager approached me. His name is Mark. He said it would be nice if one of the family could act as a guide. I thought it would be better than sitting at home on my own. So here I am. I love it. I feel like an actress."

"You won't have a job much longer," said Roy, "if the villagers go on being sullen."

"Any minute now, you'll see a change. Mark's just been round the lot handing out letters saying that if they don't smarten up their act, he's going to start charging rent. Look at the waitresses behind the counter reading theirs."

Agatha could see their startled, shocked faces. Then they were suddenly beaming and bustling about the tables.

"What about Sadie?" asked Agatha. "Was she ever up in court?"

"Didn't get that far. Good psychiatrist put the wind up the police."

"So what is she doing now?"

"Sadie and Sir Henry have bought a real manor house and are having a wonderful time."

"Do you miss Bert?"

"I did at first. It was more like losing a difficult child than a husband. But after I got this job I found I hardly ever thought of him. I still think of poor Jimmy. What a waste! He adored that nasty mother of his. I'd better go and get ready for the next tour."

She called over one of the waitresses. "Don't charge for this tea. See you, Agatha, and thanks for everything."

Roy and Agatha made their way back to the carriage. This time the driver jumped down from the box and bowed low as he helped them in.

Back in the village, the children were dancing energetically round the maypole, the Morris Men were leaping about, and Doris was spinning wool as if her life depended on it.

"Want to try the pub?" asked Roy.

"No, I want to get out of here. All this Olde English rubbish is getting on my nerves."

Back at the cottage, Roy said, "You haven't looked at your mail."

Agatha flicked through the small pile she had left on the kitchen table and stopped at an envelope with a foreign stamp. She opened it up. It was from James.

"Dear Agatha," she read. "Am here in Arles as part of my travel research. Why not come over and join me? I am staying at the Hotel Maurice in the centre. Miss you. Love, James."

Agatha stared ahead for a long moment. She felt a pang of grief for her lost obsession. Then she brightened. There were other men out there. Lots of them!

And she would marry one of them—tall, rich and handsome—and she would invite James to the wedding.

"Not that I care any more," she said aloud.

"Care about what?" asked Roy.

"About what he thinks."

"He who?"

"Never mind," said Agatha Raisin.